The Fateful Knight

ALSO BY
JANET RAYE STEVENS

The Beryl Blue Adventures in Time

Beryl Blue, Time Cop

It's Been A Long, Long Time

Every Time We Say Goodbye

Time Travel Suspense

The Titanic Time Heist

WWII Paranormal Suspense

A Moment After Dark

Contemporary Holiday Romance

Cole for Christmas

The Fateful Knight

JANET RAYE
AWARD-WINNING AUTHOR
STEVENS

GREAT BROOK PUBLISHING

Copyright © 2024 Janet Raye Stevens.

First Electronic Edition: May 2007
Second Electronic Edition: July 2024
ISBN - 978-8-9901207-1-6
First Print Edition: July 2024
ISBN - 978-8-9901207-0-9

All rights reserved. This book or any portion thereof may not be reproduced or used in any manner whatsoever without the express written permission of the publisher except for the use of brief quotations in a book review. No part of this book may be used in the formation or use of AI technologies without express permission from the author.

This is a work of fiction. Any similarity between the characters and situations within its pages and places or persons, living or dead, is unintentional and co-incidental.

Printed in the United States of America. First printing, 2024

www.janetrayestevens.com

Cover Design by Karasel Cover Art.

Now the fair goddess, Fortune,
Fall deep in love with thee, and her great charms
Misguide thy opposers' swords!
William Shakespeare, "Much Ado About Nothing"

Chapter One

"Over here, you'll see the battle armor of Sir Henry Heroux, circa 1410," the tour guide said, steering the group to a gleaming suit of armor that lurked in a corner of the spacious gallery.

Beth Astley followed as if pulled by a magnet, her gaze pasted on the guide. As a lover of all things medieval, she'd visited the Walker Museum a bazillion times in the year since she'd moved to Preston, Massachusetts. She'd lingered for hours in galleries stuffed full of armor, shields, helmets, and weaponry from around the world, some pieces dating back a thousand years. She'd taken dozens of much speedier tours as she accompanied the ninth graders in her world history classes on field trips to the museum.

And she'd even been on this midnight tour of the Great Hall a few times. Well, eight o'clock tour, actually, but the atmosphere in the cavernous room had a spooky, haunted castle at midnight feel, with its cathedral ceiling, the earthy scent of its rough stone walls, and a dozen stained-glass windows depicting knights at battle. Muted light from the massive chandeliers suspended from the rafters on thick chains spread an antique—and creepy—glow over the room.

So yeah, Beth knew every square inch of this museum, could quote every descriptive label on every exhibit and was on a first name basis with all the suits of armor arranged around the Great Hall like silent sentries.

But she'd *never* seen this particular tour guide before. *Him* she would remember. About thirty, dressed in a chest-hugging black tee shirt and butt-hugging jeans, he had a slender, muscular build, tousled raven hair, a prominent nose, rugged two-days beard growth dappling a square jaw, tanned skin, and dark blue eyes.

"We know only a few details about Sir Henry's life," the hot tour guide continued, gazing at Sir Henry's armor and dropping his voice as if he feared he might awaken the metal man. "We know he was a knight in the king's service, well respected, a fearless warrior and a fair lord. From all accounts he wasn't the most polished of men, but he managed to win the hand of a wealthy and beautiful noblewoman. A true love match. She turned down many suitors to marry him."

A young woman next to Beth, dressed in a Maid Marian outfit and a crown of flowers on her hair, sighed at the romantic tale. Though tempted to do the same, Beth suspected some embellishments in the guide's story. The true events that brought a couple of that time period together more likely involved the merger of powerful families and lots of land, with the bride having no say in the matter.

"We also know how Sir Henry died," the guide said in a hushed tone, tinged with frustration and even anger. "He was attacked and murdered on his way to meet an emissary of the king." He waited until the group's buzz of outrage simmered down before continuing. "After his death, Sir Henry's armor was broken up and the pieces scattered around England. The museum's founder made it his mission to put the armor back together. The staff here took up the cause after Mr. Walker died and over the last six years, we've managed to beg, borrow, or steal the rest of the pieces. The *couter*—" He gestured to a hinged steel pad on the metal man's elbow. "Was located a year ago, leaving only one piece missing. A crucial piece."

He stepped a little closer to Sir Henry. Beth did too, riveted.

"A knight's primary weapon of offense, and often defense, was his sword." The guide directed their gaze toward the armor's right arm and the stump of purple velvet where the gauntlet should have been. "As the story goes, Sir Henry met his opponent without his gauntlet to protect his sword hand. Without that battle glove, the knight was as vulnerable as if naked."

"Why didn't he have it?" an older man at the front of the group asked. "What happened to it?"

The guide hesitated a long time, almost as if he hadn't heard the question. Or didn't want to answer.

"Stolen? Hidden by an enemy?" he said finally. "Something supernatural, maybe." His voice dipped to a grim whisper. "If you believe in that type of thing."

A gloomy pall fell over the Great Hall. Beth shuddered, imagining the poor knight fighting for his life, and wondering what could have happened to the gauntlet to leave him so unprotected.

"Does anyone have any other questions?" Hot Tour Guide asked, breaking the silence.

"I do," a kid of about twelve piped up. "How did the knights go to the bathroom wearing those things?"

Everyone laughed, even the guide. "That's a question for another tour," he said, and the group moved on to examine a piece of tournament armor from France and then a Japanese Samurai's helmet, called a kabuto.

The tour concluded with a stroll past a gorgeous fifteenth century Russian tapestry depicting men on a hunt. The guide led the way to the exit, and like everyone else, Beth petted the statue of the museum's mascot as she passed through the door. The statue, a life-like Jack Russell terrier named Bruno, looked more adorable than fierce in his armored coat and helmet adorned with red feathers.

Beth descended the wide stone steps in the middle of the group, glad she'd taken time from the museum's annual Renaissance fair celebration outside to go on the Great Hall tour. Not everyone's idea of a hot Saturday night date, but definitely hers.

She'd almost reached the bottom step when she tripped. Stumbled over something in her path, or her own clumsy feet, she couldn't be sure.

"Watch it."

The guide spun around and grabbed her hand, halting her impending face plant. Their gazes caught, and so did Beth's breath. His eyes up close were the most amazing shade of blue, the color of a midnight sky, unsettled, stormy, as if something troubled him. Deeply.

"We've met," he said.

Not a question. A statement of fact, delivered with a heap of surprise, and a hitch of alarm.

"No, we haven't..." Her voice trailed off as he gently squeezed her hand. The chatter of voices in the stairwell and from the fairgoers outside faded into a heavy stillness. The sharp smell of sandalwood and candle smoke rose up and Beth's vision rippled like water on a pond. An ominous roll of thunder rumbled in the distance.

"My lady, I must go," the guide said, his voice different. Aching and desperate.

Beth blinked, bringing him into focus. His tousled hair had suddenly grown long, touching his shoulders. Candlelight lit his metal armor breastplate with a dull sheen. A memory tweaked inside her.

"I cannot bear to leave you," he said. "But you know I have no choice." He brushed his thumb over the back of her hand then bent and touched his lips to her wrist. Waves of pleasure washed over her, but also a sense of dread.

"Hey, what's the hold up?" a man behind her called, followed by a dozen other voices, impatient and in a hurry.

Beth snapped out of her trance and snapped her hand out of the tour guide's grip just as fast.

Before she could move or even consider what had just happened, the people behind her shoved past and down the remaining stairs to the door. They swept Beth along with the tide and moments later she stood outside near one of the fair's many booths and concessions stands.

And her knight in shining armor was gone.

Or had he never been there at all?

BETH SHOOK OFF THE RIDICULOUSNESS of that thought. She brushed off what may or may not have happened in the stairwell, too. The eeriness of the Great Hall, the sad story of Sir Henry's murder, and the heroics of one extremely good-looking tour guide keeping her from falling had sparked her overactive and overly romantic imagination.

She waded into the crowd of fairgoers spread out along the museum's broad lawn. Everyone with even the slightest interest in medieval lore had come out for the annual Renaissance fair. She passed jesters in hats with bells, men in leggings and tunics, and women wearing tall conical hats and embroidered gowns that looked as if they weighed a thousand pounds.

Beth hadn't gone all-in on the cosplay, but she had made good use of an old bridesmaid's gown for tonight's festivities. A soft, silky lavender—not exactly her best color—the dress had wide sleeves and an empire waist. A matching pair of sandals peeped out from under the hem, and she'd twisted her long, auburn hair into a braid that spilled down her back.

She stopped at one of the fair's many food carts offering a variety of delicacies from around the world. She bought a piece of fried dough and nibbled on the treat while watching a jousting demonstration without horses, just two men with lances dancing around like in a *Monty Python* movie.

After she finished, she brushed sugar off her hands and entered one of the vendor tents selling collectibles. *Alleged* collectibles, actually. Most of the items spread across tables or tossed into bins were old clothing from grandma's attic, battered beer steins, and used *Lord of the Rings* action figures. Stuff she wouldn't pay ten cents for, never mind the ten dollars for each item noted on the sign.

She lost hope of finding anything good and turned away, when she stumbled into a man who'd sauntered into the tent for a look-see—the tour guide.

The scent of sandalwood cloaked her again and Beth's thoughts shot back to the incident in the stairwell. Her cheeks roasted with embarrassment. How could she have gaped at the man like that? And imagined him kissing her wrist? Admittedly, it had been a while since she and Ty had broken up, and the few dates she'd had since moving here hadn't exactly been stellar. But to fantasize about a total stranger? No, just no.

His dark eyebrows drew down as if he'd picked up on her thoughts and he stared at her an uncomfortably long time, with that same expression of confusion and alarm as before.

She tore her gaze away from his and focused instead on the items she'd already pored over quite thoroughly.

"See anything interesting?" he asked.

Yeah, you. She kicked that thought out of her head as fast as it had arrived and picked up a toy Frodo that looked as if a baby had used it as a teething ring. "Uh...not much. I suppose everything of value's already been scooped up."

Thunder rumbled as she spoke. The wind shifted, the flaps of the vendor's tent fluttered, and something silver on the table flashed, a bit of metal peeking out from under an embroidered scarf.

The tour guide saw it at the same time she did. "Perhaps not everything." He shoved the scarf aside to reveal a gauntlet, a steel glove from a suit of armor.

He hauled in a sharp breath. Beth gasped too.

The metal glimmered in the buttery glow of the overhead lights. It seemed to be of good quality craftsmanship, but well used. Scratches crisscrossed the silvery surface and a chunk of the thumb had been broken off. Beth lifted an eyebrow. Where had that come from? She could swear it hadn't been there before.

The guide snapped his gaze toward her again. "Do you believe in fate?" he said.

Beth shivered at the intensity in his voice. "W-what?"

He frowned, like she'd given the wrong answer on a test. Like she'd completely disappointed him.

Beth squared her shoulders. Well, what did he expect when he'd thrown such a dorky pickup line at her? *Do you believe in fate* had to be right up there with *do you come here often* in the cheesy pickup line hall of fame.

"Never mind," he said and reached for the gauntlet.

Beth got to it first. Why she grabbed it, she didn't know. Something deep inside her, some kind of impulse told her to. Told her she *had* to. The glove lay palm up on the table, like a turtle on its back, and the jointed metal fingers seemed to curl around her hand as she snatched it up. The steel felt oddly warm. A sizzling charge, like an electrical surge, tingled across her skin.

The tour guide snorted. "Do you really want that? It's just a piece of junk."

"No it's not." She inspected the glove from fingertip to cuff. "I'm not an expert, but this looks like a professionally crafted piece." Like something her artist father would've made, if he worked in steel instead of the more malleable pewter. "Like, it may even be valuable."

"I *am* an expert." He flashed a scowl. An extremely hot scowl. "I'm the curator of European armor at this museum and I can tell you it's worthless. It's probably a prop from a high school production of Camelot."

He reminded Beth of her students who argued with her over their grades, as if their *the-dog-ate-my-homework* reasoning and excuses could get her to change her mind. "Hold on. If it *is* a piece of junk, why do you want it?"

"Really? You're gonna do this?" His scowl deepened and Beth felt the need to fan herself. "I saw it first."

"Ah, but I *touched* it first. And possession is nine-tenths of the law."

He stepped closer, invading her personal space. Her senses reeled from his nearness and his fresh, sandalwood scent. His expression changed. Not for the better. He looked anxious, hounded, his eyes stormy and piercing. His voice changed too, going low and hot.

"You don't understand," he bit off. "I *need* that gauntlet."

More thunder grumbled, far away, getting closer. Beth tightened her hold and the metal glove seemed to heat up even more. That vague memory that had flared into her mind on the stairwell rushed back again. Perhaps she *had* met him, in the museum or somewhere else.

Long ago.

When they'd kissed.

What?

Her cheeks burned as hot as the metal piece clutched in her hands. What was she thinking? Her brain had taken a sharp turn off the road to reality. She didn't know this man, didn't know anything about him. Except that he seemed pretty desperate to get his hands on something he'd called junk.

Well, he wasn't going to get it. She flinched out of the curator's reach. "Sorry," she said, adding one of her politest smiles. "*I* need it too."

His expression went steely, as if she'd stolen something he'd wanted forever. Beth fled toward the cash register before the guilt—and those accusing eyes—could change her mind.

THE FESTIVITIES HAD BEGUN TO WIND DOWN. Beth joined the mob of fairgoers heading for their cars in the packed parking lot. Suddenly, a barrel-chested guy of about forty, with pale, mottled skin and a Cro-Magnon forehead came out of nowhere and bashed into her. She fumbled and just barely managed to hang onto the gauntlet.

"Forgive me, my lady," the rude man said, with a curt nod of apology.

He wore a Robin Hood costume, complete with feathered cap, not an unusual sight in the vicinity of an event like this, but his deep voice and heavy accent stood out. British, she thought. If that was even him speaking. His thick black beard obscured his mouth and Beth could barely see his lips.

"That's an attractive piece," he added, his gaze dropping to the item in her hand. "I'll give you one hundred pounds for it."

Oh yeah, definitely British. At least he offered her money, unlike the curator who thought he could just use those burning laser eyes to charm it out of her hands.

"Sorry, mister, no sale." She hugged the glove tightly. The heat of the metal seared her palms. "Maybe you can find another one inside."

He growled like he wasn't about to take no for an answer. Bolts of lightning flashed across the sky like grasping fingers, followed by another foreboding roll of thunder. Fear cut through her and Beth hurried away. She dashed toward her car at full tilt.

Behind her, she heard the bearded man say, "Sweet dreams, my lady."

Odd, but relatively benign parting words—so why did that innocent phrase sound sinister?

Chapter Two

Hal Campion raced to the fair's exit gate in time to see the woman sprint across the parking lot as if her hair had suddenly caught fire. She hopped into a blue car and tore out of the lot with an ear-splitting screech of tires.

Fate, you sure have a sick sense of humor.

Only a cosmic bad joke could explain his dream woman dropping so suddenly into his life, then walking away with the one thing he'd spent so long hunting for.

She'd kept to the middle of the crowd during the tour of the Great Hall. Hal hadn't gotten a good look at her beyond the occasional swish of her skirt or flip of her braided hair. But when she'd stumbled on the stairs, and he'd reached out to steady her...

Wham.

Fate punched him in the gut.

The resemblance to Elizabeth was astonishing. In her late twenties, tall, with a curvy figure and thick, dark red hair, a heart-shaped face and a blush of pink on her fair skin, the woman looked so much like Elizabeth she could be her twin sister. She even had the same beautiful eyes. Warm and shining, glimmering with life, and as green as a blade of grass touched with dew.

She rivaled Elizabeth in her feistiness, too. She'd stolen that gauntlet from him with ease and a satisfied smile.

Hal clenched his jaw in frustration. Seeing her had iced him through and through. Seeing that elusive treasure he and so many others had spent years searching for had burned him to the core. The gauntlet seemed to have appeared out of thin air. An emotional tsunami crashed over him when he'd seen it, paralyzing him, unable to move.

Who was she? What brought her here tonight? When he'd clasped her hand on the stairs, a sizzle of energy seemed to pass between them. In the

THE FATEFUL KNIGHT

vendor's tent, she'd gazed at him as if she knew him, giving him a glimmer of hope she knew everything. That she understood what the gauntlet meant to him, understood the darkness and the dreams that had plagued him for almost a year.

The more important question—how had Sir Henry's battle glove ended up tossed onto that collectibles table like a used oven mitt in a flea market? Hal had known it was authentic the second he'd seen it. The style and design fit the rest of the knight's armor, right down to the mark of the armorer who'd designed it stamped on the cuff.

Then the woman had waltzed away with it and Hal's confusion had simmered for too many precious moments before he'd managed to shake free of his brain freeze and chase after her.

Too late. He watched the redheaded thief's car race toward the parking lot's exit, with his treasure inside.

God's teeth, now what?

Hal had finally found the one thing he desperately needed. The only thing that could stop the nightmares. The thing he'd wanted more than anything else in the world.

Except for Elizabeth.

And he'd let both slip away.

CHAPTER THREE

Beth floored the gas pedal and her car barreled down the street. The thunder died away. She cast a frantic glance in her rearview mirror, expecting to see Beard Man's hulking form storming after her. But that guy had vanished, replaced by the hot curator. He stood near the entrance gate, his gaze pinned on her car. His reflection grew smaller in her mirror as she drove away, then disappeared.

She glanced at the gauntlet on the passenger seat next to her. The curator's desperate words echoed in her mind. *I need that gauntlet.* Guilt pinched her conscience. Maybe she should have given it to him. She'd acted rashly, in the heat of the moment.

Something she did all the time then regretted later when she'd had a chance to cool down.

She touched the glove. The odd heat from earlier had dissipated and she felt only cold steel. *She* needed it too, but not for the reason her intense tour guide wanted it. He probably wanted it to play dress up or to use as an educational tool during school tours. Valid reasons, less emotional than Beth's.

She wanted it for her dad.

Beth's father had been fascinated by the romance and fantasy of all things medieval. He'd been captivated by the era, a time when mounted knights rode out to battle and their steadfast ladies waved them goodbye, when honor and chivalry were everything.

She had followed in his footsteps. She'd grown up playing with toy swords and the metal horses Dad would make for her from odds and ends in his art studio. He'd read her bedtime stories about Merlin and King Arthur, Eleanor of Aquitaine, and gallant Samurai and their trusty swords. They'd watch old movies with knights saving fair damsels and protecting people from evildoers.

He'd called her mother his beloved and Beth his little lady. And he'd eagerly encouraged her interest in history and studying the past. No surprise she'd become a high school history teacher. When he'd died two years ago, way too young, his loss had opened up a hole in both her mother's life and Beth's own. Filled with grief and regret, she'd been struggling to move forward.

Beth traced her finger over a jagged scratch in the gauntlet's smooth surface. Her throat tightened with emotion. The real reason she'd fought the hot curator for this beautiful piece of art. It represented a tangible connection, however small, to her dad.

She pulled into the parking lot of the Camelot Arms apartment complex, a place she'd chosen to live because of its name, though the architecture and layout bore no resemblance to a castle. A half dozen buildings, with four floors of box-like one- and two-bedroom apartments spread across several acres of concrete close to the highway.

The inside of her own one-bedroom box was more appealing. She'd spiffed up her living space with posters she'd bought from the Walker Museum, a not-so-good tapestry of a castle she'd woven in a college art class, and the pewter figurines of horses and knights her father had crafted.

Beth kicked off her sandals and placed the gauntlet on her desk under a framed print of a dark-haired man in armor, his helmet tucked under his arm. It may have been her imagination or overactive libido, but she thought the hot curator looked a bit like Sir Anonymous Knight in the print. The curator had a knightly thing about him, with his rugged features and his long, lean body that would wear armor well. Not to mention the smoldering intensity of a man about to face his enemies in battle.

More thunder crashed outside her windows. Beth stiffened. How strange. A thunderstorm wasn't unheard of in May, but she hadn't spotted a single cloud in the sky.

She shook off her uneasiness and poured herself a generous glass of cabernet, ending the evening with her nose buried in a book, a romantic adventure set during the Middle Ages, of course.

An hour later, she put on her comfy pajamas and crawled into bed, snuggling under the comforter. Turning on her side, she gazed at the gauntlet she'd placed on the nightstand. She caught a gleam of metal in the darkness before she closed her eyes.

In the distance, she heard the sound of thunder.

SHE PADDED DOWN WORN STONE STEPS in leather-soled shoes. She slid her hand along the cold, rough wall for balance. Wood smoke and the scent of sandalwood drifted up the stairwell from the hall below. The smell of burning wax from the candle she carried in a brass holder tickled her nose. The flame flickered as she increased her pace.

A figure rushed up toward her and stopped on the step below, bringing them eye to eye. Her breath caught. *The curator*. The same yet different, older, a bit gaunter, but still handsome. He wore a tight-fitting, long sleeve tan shirt and cotton leggings, what Beth knew a knight wore under his armor.

"Did you find it?" he asked, his British-accented voice pitched low. His blue eyes looked black in the candlelight. And frantic.

Did she find...? Beth looked down and saw she wore a loose, dark green, medieval-style linen dress, cinched at the waist with a gold girdle. Her hair trailed in a long braid over her right shoulder and lay heavily upon her breast.

Oh. I'm dreaming.

"I don't know what you mean," she began, confused, before dream knowledge kicked in and she knew what to say. "...Martha said she saw Robert playing with it several days ago. Our son yearns to be like his father. He is already training to be a warrior at six."

Our son?

A mixture of pride and frustration flashed across her dream man's face. "I allowed him to spar with it. That is what I get for being indulgent with the boy."

Anxiety squeezed her belly. "I am uneasy at your plan. I do not trust Sir Faintree. You know as well as I he is not an honorable man. He claims he has asked you to meet him under orders from the king. I fear the request is a ruse. Why else would he demand you come alone? He means to draw you out and kill you."

He dismissed that with a wave. "Do not think I trust that villain enough to meet him unprotected. I will have my armor." He slapped his thigh. "I need that cursed gauntlet."

"Henry," she said softly. "I could not bear it if something should happen to you."

He took her hand and pressed his lips to her wrist. "Hush, my lady. We have always known I must face him someday. Faintree is ambitious. And still resentful that you married me and not him."

"I could not like him from the moment we met."

"Your refusal fuels his anger even now, ten years on." His lips curved in a teasing grin. "He still covets your land."

Her mood lightened a little and she smiled. "Am I so unappealing, husband? Sir Faintree wanted me for my land only? I suppose if not for my dowry, you would never have agreed to wed."

His earthy scent enveloped her as he came up on the step beside her. She tipped her head back to meet his eyes. His smile faded and his expression filled with passion.

"You know why I married you." He cupped her face with both hands and brushed her cheeks with his thumbs. A supple, dreamy ache spread through Beth's body. "When I return, I shall thoroughly remind you, my dear Elizabeth."

He took her into his arms and leaned in for a kiss. She parted her lips, eager to taste him, eager to feel his mouth on hers...

Beth jerked awake.

What a moment to wake up. And what a dream. Inspired, no doubt, by her encounter with the hot curator and a guilty conscience for thieving the gauntlet right out from under his nose. The most realistic dream she'd ever had, almost like a memory. She touched her cheek. She still felt the dream man's tender caress on her skin, the strength of his arms around her, the warmth of his body pressed against her. The heat of his lips touching hers.

Stretching languidly, she turned on her left side. Something poked her cheek. Her eyes flew open. The gauntlet. On her pillow. She must've thrashed around so much in her sleep she'd pulled it from the nightstand onto her bed.

One of those metal fingers could put her eye out if she wasn't careful, so for safety's sake, she took the glove to the living room and placed it on her desk, under the poster of the dark-haired knight. A perfect fit.

Beth got a drink, then went back to bed and tried to sink into that hot dream again, hoping for a chance to finish that kiss.

But her subconscious had other plans.

She tugged a brass ring to open the door and stepped outside into the midday sun. The summer's warmth kissed her face, her linen undergarments brushed sensuously against her skin as she walked. The aroma of wood smoke, horse dung, and other ripe scents filled the air. Voices rose and fell. Children laughed.

Somehow Beth knew the dream had taken her to the outer ward of Elizabeth and Sir Henry's manor. The thick, protective stone wall loomed at her back and a winding path stretched in front of her, flanked on both sides by small, thatch-roofed buildings and farm fields, lush with new growth. The road disappeared into the ominous darkness of a forest in the distance.

She moved to the center of the ward, joining men, women, and children of all ages dressed in rough wool garments and caps, people who'd come to see Sir Henry off. They murmured anxiously, shifting from foot to foot.

A stout, grizzled man approached. Though dressed in garments of a finer cut than the others, his expression mirrored their concern. Village gossip had assured everyone knew the threat Sir Henry faced on this journey.

"Geraint," Beth said, greeting Henry's steward with a nod. Her voice trembled with worry. "Is my lord ready?"

"Aye." Geraint glanced to his left. "He comes from the stables."

The hot curator...Henry, actually...rode into view on the back of a massive, muscled horse. He spurred the beast up a small incline toward her. Beth's breath caught. He wore the battle armor she'd seen in the museum, thick breastplate, mail skirt, metal tassets to protect his thighs, calf-hugging greaves and steel sabaton covering his feet. His helmet sat in front of him on his saddle's pommel. His sheathed sword hung from his hip.

The only thing missing was protection for his sword hand.

He tugged the reins. His horse stopped with a snort. Henry gazed down at her with a reassuring smile that did not reach his eyes.

"My lady," he said, his voice so heavy her heart lurched. "I am off."

Please don't go, Beth's brain screamed. *Stay here with me.* The words remained unspoken. She knew he must go. He knew his duty. He'd promised to meet Sir Faintree, and a knight always kept his word.

A chubby-cheeked boy of six, with dark raven curls dashed up beside her. Their son, Robert. Beth lifted him and his father enveloped the boy in a bruising hug before releasing him into Geraint's meaty arms.

Everyone fell back, leaving Beth alone with her knight. Dread pooled in her belly as she reached up to hold Henry's hand. He wore only a leather glove that felt so thin. So vulnerable.

"Take care, my love," Beth said. "Come back to me."

He squeezed her hand, a brief touch, and spurred his horse. She shielded her eyes from the sun, watching him gallop down the path, past the houses and fields. Sunlight winked off his armor as he rode at a steady pace toward the gloom of the forest.

Thunder echoed on the horizon as her husband disappeared from sight.

Suddenly, a stable boy rushed up. "My lady," he cried, excited and out of breath. "Look! My lord's squire found this near the sheep's pen. Said it came out of nowheres."

The boy dropped to one knee. He held Henry's gauntlet.

Geraint returned to her side. "He only just left, my lady," he said. "I shall bring it to him."

She looked fondly at Geraint then at her son, seated contentedly on the steward's shoulders, his hands fisted in Geraint's remaining wisps of hair.

"No. You keep watch here," she said. "Alert the men to be on guard for any of Sir Faintree's tricks."

She knew what she had to do. Henry's desperate plea echoed in her mind. *I need that gauntlet.* Without it, he would die.

She plucked the battle glove from the stable boy's hands. "Bring me my horse. I'm going to find my husband."

Moments later, Beth galloped down the road as if the devil himself bit at her heels. The wind cooled her face and tugged at her braid. She'd thrown a heavy cloak over her green dress when she set out, the gauntlet held fast in one of its deep pockets.

In dream time, she arrived at her destination in mere seconds, though she knew the journey had taken much longer. She twitched the reins. Her horse slowed as she turned off the path and picked her way along a barely-there trail into a thick forest.

Beth shuddered. She didn't like the woods, not since she'd gotten lost in Dale Park when she was six. Dream her didn't like the forest either. Too dark, too many places for an enemy to hide.

A far-off neigh cut through the trees. *Henry*.

She urged her mount in that direction. She trotted into the clearing and her heart lifted. She'd found him.

She hurled herself from her horse, snatched the gauntlet from her pocket and started toward him. The thud of hooves beating the ground broke the stillness around them.

Henry seized her gaze. "Elizabeth, go back. I beg you. You are in danger here."

The thunder of riders approaching grew louder, bearing down on them. The gauntlet Beth held warmed, then heated to boiling...

A flock of blackbirds let out a fierce squawk. Henry and the clearing dissolved. The sounds and smells of the forest faded. Beth eased out of the dream. She blinked away the cobwebs of sleep and came back to the twenty-first century.

The blackbirds wailed again, or, rather, her phone, chirping like an angry bird. Her mother calling for their weekly chat, or maybe her friend Sheila, checking in about book club on Wednesday, or someone else dedicated to waking Beth up way too early on a Sunday morning and dragging her from her dream.

She groaned in annoyance. She wanted to know what happened next. Was *desperate* to know.

She turned to reach for the phone on the nightstand—and froze. The morning sun slipped around the window curtains and streamed across her bed.

The sunlight brushed across the gauntlet, resting on her pillow.

Chapter Four

*T*onight, Hal dropped directly into the nightmare, skipping over the good parts of the dream—the lingering kiss on the stairs, saying goodbye to Robert, Sir Henry's precious last moments with Elizabeth. Instead, Hal found himself facing the frantic seconds before the attack began.

Panting almost as much as his horse from their hard ride, Hal as Henry trotted into the clearing, where he and Sir Faintree were supposed to meet. He dismounted and his boots hit the hard-packed earth with a thump. He tethered his horse to a tree stump as he always did. He peeled off his helmet and rested it in a dip on the moss-speckled boulder where he always put it.

THE FATEFUL KNIGHT

And, as he did each time he got caught in this nightmare, he surveyed his surroundings.

He stood in an open area surrounded by a tangle of trees and overgrown brush. Sunlight struggled through the tree branches and dappled the ground with flickering spots of light. A carpet of leaves and moss covered the soil. The scent of earth hung heavily in the air. A warm mist danced over the tree roots that bumped up from the ground.

A fine place for a tryst.

Or to meet an enemy bent on betrayal.

Hal removed his flask from a saddle pouch and drank. Mead, or wine, or something else he'd never been able to identify, no matter how many times he relived this moment. Funny. He could smell, hear, see, and feel everything around him in the dream, in hyper-realistic detail. But he couldn't taste a thing.

He dropped his flask at the snap of a twig in the trees. His gut tightened when a white horse emerged from the path, with Elizabeth sitting tall and proud on its back. Hope sparked in the breast of the man Hal inhabited, but Hal knew only horror.

He'd lived through this moment time and time again. He dreaded what happened next.

"Henry," she called, her voice filled with relief. She jumped off her horse, looped the reins around a low branch, and pulled the gauntlet from a pocket of her cloak. "I have what you need."

She started across the clearing toward him. The rumble of horses approaching suddenly shook the ground. Several riders headed their way, closing in on the clearing.

Icicles of terror sprinted down Hal's spine. "Elizabeth, go back," he said, with Sir Henry's voice. "I beg you. You are in danger here."

The drum of hoofbeats drew closer. Men shouted. Elizabeth froze, her frightened gaze on Hal. With the hopeless movements of a doomed man, he took the helmet from the rock shelf. The world went dark as he put it on. He lifted the visor so he could see, but still his range of vision was limited.

Three enormous horses pounded into the clearing. Their riders brandished thick swords they swung with abandon. Only one man wore

THE FATEFUL KNIGHT

armor—Sir Faintree. Hal unsheathed his sword. Elizabeth had been right not to trust the man. This was an ambush.

Hal moved to protect Elizabeth, but Faintree's minions flung themselves from their horses and muscled between them. One of villains threw Elizabeth to the ground and pounced on her, digging his knee into her back. She shrieked and fought with vigor, struggling to throw the man off.

Faintree dismounted as fast as anyone in armor could get off a horse and he and the other man came at Hal. Sparks flew and metal zinged against metal as Hal tried to fight them off. As always, he scored a hit right away on Faintree's man. The man fell, mortally wounded.

One down, two to go.

"Give way, Sir Faintree," Hal cried, his voice muffled behind his helmet. A hopeful but futile demand. Faintree would never give way. This duel would be to the death.

His opponent laughed, a nasty, corrosive sound, and doubled his attack. He lunged with swift, violent strokes. Hal parried mightily but fell back toward the boulder. Once there, he'd be trapped, no way to escape.

He needed his gauntlet. *Now.*

He risked a glance at Elizabeth, on the ground nearby. She held the battle glove under her, while attempting to escape her captor's hold. That pig jabbed his knee deeper into her spine and seized her braid, yanking her head back. He pressed his short sword to her throat.

"No, you fool!" Faintree cried. "Don't kill her. I *want* her."

Hal took advantage of the distraction. With a blood-chilling howl, he surged at his foe and did something he'd never done before, in all the nights he'd been locked in this dream battle. He wrested control from fate and fought dirty. He swung his sword like a baseball bat and the flat of his blade struck Faintree's helmet with a reverberating *ting*. The man staggered like a drunkard.

Hal smirked. *All's fair in love and war, right?*

He spun to rush to Elizabeth's aid, hoping he'd somehow changed destiny. That he'd made the dream different. Hoping *this* time, he could save her.

His foe rallied, dashing his hopes. Faintree's sword seemed to flash at the speed of light as he swung with a mighty force—and sliced off Hal's hand.

It took a fraction of a second for the pain to hit, like a space between heartbeats. Then, a bitter, biting heat shuddered from his wrist and shot through his body on a titanic wave. A throat-scorching scream tore from his mouth. A flock of crows waiting to pick over the remains of the battle's loser flapped away, squawking in protest at the sound.

Faintree came in for the kill. His blade found the chink in Hal's armor and sank into his breastbone with a sharp, fatal thrust.

"Henry! No," Elizabeth cried, an anguished wail.

Wincing in agony, Hal dropped to his knees. Blood poured from his wounds. His vision dimmed, and his ears rang as his life seeped from his veins. Through the haze he found Elizabeth and locked his eyes on her.

She wriggled under her captor's imprisoning knee and managed to snatch her dagger from its sheath on her hip. She stabbed the man in the thigh. He howled and then...

The end of this torturous dream. The nightmare he'd lived almost every night, playing out to its morbid conclusion. The thing he couldn't stop no matter how much he tried. Like so many aspects of his waking life he'd been unable to control. His brutal childhood. His parents' neglect and constant fighting. His brother's slow slide into alcoholism. His own inability to put the past behind him and move forward.

And that redheaded thief who'd snatched his treasure out from under his nose.

The dreams had started nearly a year ago, after Hal's team had located the next to the last piece of Sir Henry's armor, with only the battle glove still missing. He had no idea why or what had triggered the nightmares, a curse, fate, or plain old-fashioned bad luck.

Whatever the cause, he knew, somehow, securing the gauntlet would be the key to escaping his torment. To breaking free from his almost nightly trip back to the early fifteenth century. To stopping him from repeatedly living Sir Henry's final moments like an endless rerun of a gruesome horror movie.

And, most of all, if he found that elusive piece of armor, it would put a blessed end to watching what happened next to his beloved Elizabeth.

Until then, the nightmare would hold him captive. Until then, he wouldn't wake until he watched the brute with his knee in Elizabeth's back draw his blade across her neck—and slit her throat.

Chapter Five

*T*he day dawned bright and warm. Attendance at the Renaissance fair had tripled from the previous night's turnout and the parking lot overflowed. Beth found a spot by the curb more than a block away and walked to the museum from there.

She'd left the gauntlet at home. After what happened last night, she'd decided they needed some time apart.

The dreams had spooked her. But finding that thing on her pillow twice in one night had creeped her out completely. She'd convinced herself she'd been so desperate to get the gauntlet to Henry in her dream that she'd sleepwalked to the desk and brought it back to her bed. But she couldn't shake the feeling that the damned thing had somehow propelled itself onto her pillow.

The Walker Museum loomed ahead, towering over the fair's tents and displays ranged along the manicured lawn. The museum's founder, Walter Walker, had been rich enough to do what Beth wished she could do but couldn't ever hope to on a teacher's salary. He'd collected thousands of pieces of art and armor from the medieval era then built his collection a fine home, a massive, castle-like stone structure on a hill, complete with parapets, a tower, and a retractable iron grate over the entrance. Her first thought when she'd moved here and had seen this magnificent building—what, no moat?

Beth paid at the gate and entered the fairgrounds. She hadn't planned to come here today, but her restless night and the glove's strange antics had sparked a few questions about Sir Henry someone who worked at the museum might be able to answer. Anyone but the hot curator. She didn't think she could look him in the eye after giving him a starring role in her dreams last night.

She bought a piece of the fried dough she was fast becoming addicted to and wended through the exhibits, passing the time until the long line of people waiting to get into the museum thinned out.

The metal ring of swords drew her to a group circled around two men fencing with sturdy, blunt-tipped epees. Dressed in padded jackets, knickers, and protective masks, the men danced in a semi-circle as they sparred, in a skilled ballet of footwork and finesse.

She couldn't peel her gaze away from the taller man, who had a lean body, muscular arms, and powerful thighs. More skilled than his foe, he parried and thrust as if he'd been fencing his whole life. He quickly disarmed his sparring partner, to hearty cheers and clapping from the onlookers. Including Beth. The men swished their swords in acknowledgement of the applause then shook hands.

The fencers strolled toward the museum's side entrance, but the taller one seemed to change his mind and turned back, heading for a refreshment table for a drink—next to where Beth stood.

Still holding his epee, he pulled off his mask and ran a hand through his raven hair, tangling it beyond control. He grabbed a cup and lifted it to his lips.

He swung his gaze toward Beth. Her belly tickled as an energetic flock of butterflies took flight inside. Every hot second of last night's dream flared into her mind. The first dream, the one with the almost kiss in the stairwell, not the second stressful one.

Do you believe in fate?

Yes, she did, at the moment. Fate, and a bit of coincidence, that she'd never seen him before yesterday, and now she kept running into him. The sexy fencing man was the curator from last night. The man she'd stolen the gauntlet from.

Her dream knight.

Chapter Six

*H*al gulped in surprise, then choked on the water he'd just drunk. *Her*. Standing there, staring at him. She looked beautiful in a summery dress and sandals, her red hair loose and free, and looking so much like Elizabeth his heart stuttered.

Maybe fate had chosen to be on his side for a change. He'd been scrambling for ideas on how to find his mystery thief, and here she was. She stepped closer. Tensing, he put down the cup and squeezed the grip of his sword, struggling to get hold of the flood of feelings raging through him.

"I guess you remember me," she said, her voice as smooth as liquid chocolate and touched with a hint of remorse.

THE FATEFUL KNIGHT

"How could I forget you? You stole something important from me." He had to find some way to steal it back or she could haunt his dreams forever.

"Ouch. You don't sugar coat things, do you?"

"Not when there's something I need. Do you have it?"

"No, it's at home." She paused and a mystified smile touched her lips. "Well, I *hope* it's at home. I wouldn't put it past the thing to have chased me all the way here."

Hal arched an eyebrow. She was joking. He thought. "So, you just came here to taunt me?"

"That's kind of arrogant. How was I supposed to know you'd be here at the fair?" She looked him over, head to toe, her expression playful. "And dressed like that. Most people look like ghostly ninja turtles in those fencing clothes, but you look pretty good. And you fence really well."

Hal laughed, surprised by her bluntness. He hadn't laughed in a long time. He thought he'd forgotten how.

"Well, I practice a lot." Thanks to his almost nightly sparring with Sir Faintree. "You should tell our fencing master you think I'm good." He checked first to make sure no one stood in stabbing range then flicked his epee in a whooshing figure eight. Like Sir Knight of the Nerds. "She says I move like a camel with four left feet. Says I might survive a real fight. Emphasis on the *might*."

His humor faded. He might survive a duel in real life, but he'd lost, every single time, in his dream showdowns.

"I took our fencing master's words as a challenge to work harder," he said, showing off some more. He lunged forward and stabbed the air. He'd trained and practiced, more motivated by his desire to defeat Faintree than impressing his coach or any of his sparring partners. "I'm pretty good with four different kinds of swords now." He placed the epee point down, gripping the hilt tightly, and peered at her. "Much as I enjoy bragging about my skills, let's talk about you. What's your name? I mean, I can't keep thinking of you as the gauntlet stealing damsel."

Though, damsel kind of fit her. Especially as she shared Elizabeth's timeless beauty, looking as if she could have stepped out of one of the tapestries in the museum's main gallery upstairs.

"I'm Beth. Beth Astley."

His eyebrows shot up. *Beth*. As in, Elizabeth. "I'm Hal Campion." He offered his hand. She gripped it with soft, smooth fingers. "Now that I know your name, Beth Astley, any chance you'll reconsider? About the gauntlet, I mean."

She tipped her head, studying him. "Why is that thing so important to you? Yeah, I get that you're into this whole Camelot thing, like me. Maybe more than me, since you work here. And I'll admit, it's beautifully crafted, but as you said, it's nothing more than a prop from some play." She hesitated. "It's not like it's real or anything. Is it?"

Their gazes locked and he almost told her. Almost blurted out the truth. That he'd known it was authentic right away and not only because the artisanship matched the rest of Sir Henry's battle gear upstairs in the gallery, but because of the dreams. Living in Henry Heroux's skin nearly every night had given Hal an up close and personal familiarity with the armor a Renaissance fair cosplayer could only dream of.

He shifted away from her and looked at the banner with the museum's knight logo hanging from a nearby streetlight. It snapped in the steady breeze. He couldn't tell her about the dreams. She'd never believe him.

"Listen, do you have a minute?" he said, avoiding her question. He tipped his head toward the side entrance. "Will you come into the museum with me?"

She looked uncertain but agreed, following him inside and up the stairs. He tossed her a glance as they reached the step where he'd touched her hand last night and that spark of energy passed between them. If she hadn't stumbled, he might not have noticed her. If fate hadn't stepped in.

"How long have you been a curator here?" she asked as they entered the Great Hall. She spoke softly. So did the rest of the visitors thronging the room, as if afraid a raised voice would disturb the silent army of armored men standing guard along the walls.

"Six years, since college," he said. "But I've spent most of my life here. I remember coming to the museum the first time when I was twelve, on a school trip. I never left." He shrugged. "I didn't have the best childhood. This place became my escape."

A place that encouraged his imagination, with people who didn't vilify his thirst to learn. An environment he could control. He pushed away the bitter memories, surprised he'd blurted that out. Or maybe not so surprised. He knew her. Really well. At least in his dreams. No wonder he felt comfortable talking with her.

"What about you?" He steered her past the jousting display that nearly filled the center of the gallery—two mannequins in authentic armor and carrying lances, mounted on white horses decked out in specialized equine battle gear. "What sparked your interest in history and this time period?"

"My dad." Affection bubbled in her voice. "He loved all this stuff. My mom, not so much. But I've been into the romance and the drama of the medieval world since I was a kid. The pageantry, the feeling that magic could be real, and anything might happen. Don't get me wrong, I'd never want to live in that time. For starters, hygiene and medicine was pretty poor, and I mean, the plague?"

He found himself laughing again. And thinking he may have found his nerdy soul mate, with or without her connection to his dreams. "Yeah, there were a lot of downsides no one wants to talk about." They'd reached Sir Henry, staring out from his corner like a lost soul. "*This* is what the crowd wants to see. The armor and what it represents. That's why stories about medieval times are so popular. Why people love festivals like this weekend's and all that. Why I love fencing."

"And why someone would move here. I jumped when I was offered a teaching job in this city. Now I can come to the museum all the time."

"Does your dad come to visit? Have you brought him here? What does he think?"

Her face freeze-framed and Hal kicked himself for bringing up an obviously painful subject.

"He never got here," she said. "He died two years ago."

"I'm sorry."

"Yeah. That's my biggest regret, really. Well, one of my biggest regrets. We'd gone out to lunch, and he had a heart attack an hour after I dropped him at home. I've always wondered, if things had been different, if I had ordered dessert or we took a longer route home, could I have saved him?"

Sadness threaded her voice and Hal fought the impulse to take her into his arms to comfort her. He reminded himself she wasn't Elizabeth. He could do that with his dream woman, not someone he barely knew.

"I get why you think that," he said instead, his tone sympathetic. "But I guess the universe had other ideas."

She nodded. "You really believe in this fate thing, don't you?"

"Beth, you have no idea."

She met his eyes. The overhead light bathed her in an almost ethereal glow, turning her hair to fire. Hal's heartbeat picked up. Heat and a sensation as old as time passed between them. It had nothing to do with his dreams and everything to do with chemistry. A natural attraction drawing him to her. Drawing them both together. They stood there, frozen, gazing at each other in silence, not a sound except for their breathing and the occasional child's squeal echoing from the gallery.

She broke away first, turning to look at Sir Henry. "Is this what you wanted to show me? You know I saw this armor last night. It's so sad that he was murdered."

"His wife Elizabeth was murdered too."

"Elizabeth?" Her face went pale. She reached out as if to touch the armor. Hal prepped a *no touching* lecture, but she halted with her hand inches from the shiny breastplate. "She was bringing him the gauntlet, wasn't she?"

Hal stilled. "How do you know that?"

She chewed her bottom lip, as if thinking up an answer. "I teach history at the high school. I've been here on dozens of field trips. I must've heard that information on one of the tours. Or perhaps I read it on the exhibit labels."

THE FATEFUL KNIGHT

Hal let that pass, despite his skepticism. He'd never mentioned Elizabeth on any of his tours, though maybe one of the docents had.

"What about the armor?" she asked. "Why was it broken up and spread around so far and wide? Did people at that time think it was... haunted?"

That question would've made any other museum employee laugh. Not him. He'd been trying to find the answer to why the armor had been separated and scattered as if it possessed dark magic since the dreams began.

"There are lots of stories about ghosts and curses and magic," he said vaguely. "Merlin and that kind of thing. It's all part of medieval lore. It would make sense if there was some superstitious legend attached to a man betrayed and murdered as Henry was. Maybe he swore revenge on his killer. Even the most educated people back then would fear such a curse. There's been some speculation his armor was deliberately broken up, so his spirit couldn't return."

She trembled.

"But that's supernatural fiction," he added quickly, somewhat spooked himself. "Only a story. The real reason is probably more boring. Each piece had a value and could've been sold dozens of times over. Now we've got Sir Henry put back together. Except one piece. We haven't even had a nibble on its whereabouts for a long time." He slid his gaze from the armor to her. "Until yesterday."

She stiffened. "Wait. You said that it wasn't real."

"I lied." He shrugged. "Sorry, but it's the real deal."

Beth's manner abruptly changed. Her eyes narrowed and her expression turned brittle. "Then how did it end up for sale with half priced Lord of the Rings action figures?"

"I don't know." Any more than he knew how it seemed to pop onto the table like it had been beamed from a starship. Or why he'd had the dreams. It was all above his pay grade. And as confusing as hell. "I only know it's real and it belongs here in the museum. With Sir Henry. Will you bring it to me?"

"Just like that? First you lie to me that it's a piece of junk, then you say it's valuable and you expect me to hand it over?"

Disappointment and anger stung Hal's heart. He'd been filling his soft brain with thoughts of her beauty and fate bringing them together and all that ox dung about them being soulmates, when she only wanted money. She didn't get the meaning and significance of that piece of armor, especially its importance to him.

"Okay, how much do you want for it?" he demanded.

She flinched and drew herself up. "Do you think me so mercenary?"

"I don't know. I don't know you at all."

"Clearly."

She turned to leave. Hal stopped her. He took her hand and held it, as gentle as Sir Henry in the dreams. "Wait, Beth. Be reasonable. It belongs here. You know that."

She huffed. "I think the gauntlet would beg to differ." She looked down at his hand holding hers then back up at his face, her green eyes filled with confusion and a bit of fear. "*It* seems to think it belongs on my pillow."

With a violent shake, she broke free of his hold and fled. Her footsteps echoed off the high ceiling as she raced across the Great Hall to the door.

"I need that gauntlet, Beth," he shouted after her. "And I'll get it any way I can."

Chapter Seven

*B*eth fumed all the way home. Not at Hal. At herself.

She squeezed the steering wheel with both hands and mentally chided herself with six hundred and one articulate and reasoned and impressively pedantic S.A.T. words for her wayward thoughts back there in the gallery. When she and Hal had gazed at each other in that deep and intense way, a strange yet familiar sensation had flooded her veins.

Do you believe in fate?

Practically his first words to her. She'd thought it a pickup line at the time, but now it made sense. She'd just met the guy, yet somehow she knew they were destined to be together.

How else could she explain the palpable energy that buzzed between them? That fiery, consuming sensation that went deeper than mere physical attraction? He felt it too, if those stinging looks he'd given her were any indication. An intense pull that begged for them to come together in a kiss.

Then Hal's lies had gotten in the way.

She knew how important the gauntlet was to him, she should've told him she'd hand it over, instead of getting into a snit and storming off. But he'd lied to her. That triggered both her anger and a lot of painful memories. Her ex-boyfriend Ty had lied to her all the time. *All. The. Time.* She vowed never to get involved with a guy like that again. She wanted someone who'd tell the truth, no matter what. A man she could trust, fully.

It seemed Hal Campion was *not* that man.

Beth steered into the Camelot Arms' parking lot. She spotted a police vehicle in front of one of the apartment buildings. *Her* building.

Anxious and concerned, she hopped from her car as soon as she pulled into her designated space and dashed toward the scene. The police car's lights flashed dully in the afternoon light and its radio squawked through the open windows. Two uniformed cops spoke with one of the first-floor residents, Mrs. Parkhurst, a sixtyish woman wearing a floral print blouse and leggings.

Beth sidled up to one of her neighbors who'd gathered to watch the action, Mariel Lenz, a bank teller who lived two doors down from her. "Mariel, what happened? I hope no one's been hurt."

Mariel shook her head, making her dangling earrings dance. "Not that serious. Somebody tried to break in through a first-floor window."

Serious enough. Camelot Arms resembled a castle fortress in name only. Little security, flimsy door locks, and the puddle that formed in the basement storage room after a heavy rainstorm was the closest thing to a moat.

"That's terrible. Nothing stolen I hope?" Beth said, worrying about the gauntlet, now that she knew how valuable it was. And how important it was to Hal.

"Nah." Mariel waved dismissively. "The guy didn't even get into the building. Mrs. Parkhurst stopped him. Smacked him with her broom and he ran off."

"Good for her," Beth said and tuned into the conversation between the police and Mrs. Parkhurst, who held a stout-handled broom and gestured animatedly with her free hand as she spoke.

"He ran off, around the corner, I think," she said. "I dunno, but it looked almost like he vanished into thin air."

The police officers shifted their feet, looking mighty skeptical, and some of the onlookers snickered, but Beth snapped to attention. An uncomfortable prickle crawled along her skin, doubling in intensity as Mrs. Parkhurst described the would-be thief. Barrel-chested, bushy eyebrows—and a thick black beard.

Could that be the man with the British accent who'd accosted her as she left the fair last night? Had he followed her somehow, looking for the gauntlet? Or could the housebreaker's resemblance to the guy who'd offered to buy it from her be a coincidence? *Another* coincidence?

The urge to call a certain hot curator came over her as she went inside. If only to yell at Hal for lying to her. If he'd been honest from the start, she would've given the gauntlet to him and she wouldn't have it anymore. She wouldn't have to worry about someone breaking into her building and scaring her neighbors. And her.

That piece of armor had turned out to be more trouble than it was worth.

BETH FINISHED GRADING THE LAST of her students' essays on art and fashion during the Renaissance and closed her laptop. She slipped the computer into her tote bag, next to the gauntlet she'd wrapped in what seemed like sixteen yards of bubble wrap. Safe and secure and ready to travel to its new home. After much consideration and even more stress over the bearded thief, she'd decided to bring it to Hal tomorrow and be done with it.

She picked up her bag—heavier than usual with several pounds of haunted metal inside—and placed it by the front door. Then she packed her lunch and ended the day as she always did, with a glass of wine and a good book. She opted for something contemporary tonight. That moody, fourteenth century-set sword-and-sorcery novel she'd been reading last night had probably influenced her strange dreams as much as the stories Hal had told during the tour or anything else.

Ah, yes, the dreams. She'd told Hal she'd heard about Elizabeth bringing Henry the gauntlet on a museum tour. She hoped that was true. She didn't want to consider any other explanation for her to have dreamed something so vivid and historically accurate.

She polished off the wine and yawned. Unable to keep her eyes open, Beth put down her book and crawled into bed around ten, a bit earlier than usual.

The dream came soon after she fell into the blissful folds of sleep...

She drifted down the manor's stairwell and moved into Henry's embrace in a languid fog. They kissed, a sweet sensation that ended too soon and she found herself transported to the outer ward. Fear weighed her down like lead as she said goodbye to her knight.

The gauntlet appeared in her hands and the dream sharpened. She galloped along the road like hellfire, her cloak whipping in the wind. She turned onto the path through the woods in the space of a breath. She trotted into the clearing. She found Henry. He called out to her, warning her to go. She fumbled with the folds of her cloak and retrieved the gauntlet, starting toward him.

Then, the hard thump of hooves. Seconds later, three riders crashed into the clearing and threw themselves from their horses—two scruffy men in coarse wool clothing, carrying short swords, and a larger man in armor, wielding a deadly-looking broadsword. He wore a helmet so she couldn't see his face, but the woman she inhabited in the dream knew without a doubt he was Henry's rival and mortal foe.

Sir Faintree.

Beth's breath hitched as Faintree and one of his men attacked Henry. The other man raced toward her. He grabbed her by the neck with a meaty hand and shoved her down on the ground before she could blink. He jabbed his knee into her back. She choked and gagged—the man and a bathtub were deadly enemies. His foul stench clouded her senses. He snatched her braid and yanked her head back.

She kept her gaze pinned on Henry, locked in combat with the two men. He took down the first man with ease, but Faintree's bulk and his skill with the sword proved a greater threat. And Henry was painfully vulnerable.

Beth wriggled and pushed, trying to free herself, trying to get to Henry. She gripped the scalding gauntlet in one hand, while struggling to reach her dagger with the other. Her captor's knee held her down. He twisted her braid and pressed his short sword to her throat.

She bit her tongue to keep from crying out and distracting Henry. He fought the battle of his life. Henry scored a hit, but Faintree rallied. A fast slice

THE FATEFUL KNIGHT

of his sword took off Henry's hand at the wrist, quickly followed by a hard thrust between the ribs.

Henry screamed, and so did she as her knight dropped to his knees. Blood poured over his breastplate. She could just make out his eyes through his helmet's visor, his gaze on her, his expression defeated, grief-stricken.

"Elizabeth..." he called weakly. Dying.

Her heart split, and darkness shrouded her soul. The gauntlet scorched her fingers, burning to the bone. It fueled her fury. She managed to free her dagger. She swung wildly and plunged the cold steel into her captor's leg. He yowled and wrenched her head back so hard she thought her neck would snap. Faintree's shouts for him to stop went unheeded.

A sharp sting seared her skin as the villain swiped his blade across her throat...

Beth fought through the clouds of sleep and terror and ripped out of her nightmare. She jerked upright and screamed, but nothing came out. Drenched in sweat, bathed in fear, her temples throbbed, and her heart drummed wildly.

She squeezed something sizzling hot and heavy in her hands, holding it like a lifeline.

The gauntlet.

Chapter Eight

Beth took the menacing, burning thing in her arms and flung it away with all her might. It sailed across the room and clattered to the floor at the foot of her bureau.

Scrambling to her feet, she stumbled on trembling legs to her tote bag by the door. It hadn't been touched or moved even an inch from where she'd left it. The sleepwalking excuse wouldn't explain how the gauntlet got into her bed this time.

She screwed up her courage and peeped into the bag. A cocoon of bubble wrap wound around a hollow, glove-shaped empty space. Beth's blood turned to ice. The ghostly gauntlet had somehow escaped its bubble wrap prison and reappeared in her hands.

She sank into a chair at her kitchen table so she wouldn't fall. She stared vacantly. Her body shook uncontrollably. Impossible. *Im*-possible. She glanced toward the bedroom and could see the glove on the floor, a muted shimmer in the dim light. An inanimate piece of metal that seemed to pulse with dark energy.

She shuddered. The treasure she'd drooled over and fought the hot curator for when she'd found it only yesterday had turned into a horrifying albatross.

She had to get rid of it.

Beth threw a robe over her pajamas and snatched the glove off the floor. She shoved it into a cardboard box plucked from her recycling bin. She used an entire roll of duct tape to seal the box, winding it around and around a dozen times, just to be sure, then she grabbed her keys and dashed down the front stairs, headed for her car.

At the front door, she grabbed the handle and a piercing static charge zapped her fingers. The sparks lit the foyer in an eerie flash. Beth snatched her hand away.

No. You won't win that easily.

Gritting her teeth, she tried again. Electricity shivered through her fingers and heated her skin to boiling, but she hung onto the handle and managed to open the door. Her slippers scuffed over the dusty, pebble strewn pavement as she hurried across the parking lot toward her car. She intended to lock the creepy thing in the trunk where it would stay until she could bring it to Hal.

An ominous rumble rose up near her car. The back of her neck prickled. Real thunder? Or the pounding of hooves from her dreams?

Terrified, she spun away from her car and dashed toward the row of trash receptacles at the edge of the parking lot. The thunder dissipated by the time she got there. She reached to open the hinged door on the side of one of the dumpsters. Her hands shook and she had trouble getting a grip on the handle.

She finally flicked open the latch and flung the door wide. The stench of old pizza, fish, and rotting eggs rushed out. Holding her nose, she pitched the box inside. She slammed the metal door with a bang that reverberated in the night. Beth wasn't taking any chances, though. She found a heavy piece of wood, a side rail from an old bed, and dragged it over to the dumpster, shoving it under the latch to keep the door securely closed.

There. Try and get out of *that* trap.

Back upstairs, she kicked off her slippers and flopped onto the sofa, shivering violently from head to toe. The dream haunted her, but not as much as the gauntlet. Hal may have claimed there was nothing supernatural about Sir Henry's armor, but that thing hadn't walked across *his* apartment and leapt into bed with him.

Yawning, she checked her phone. Three-thirty. She couldn't disturb Hal now, but as soon as dawn broke, she would call him and tell him to come get his spooky glove. He'd have to dumpster dive to find it, but too bad.

Until he got here, she would stay awake. She yawned again. She could do that. No way would she be able to fall back asleep, anyway. Maybe she should make a pot of coffee.

THE FATEFUL KNIGHT

The dream took hold the moment Beth closed her eyes...

She drifted from the stairwell to the outer ward, to her horse, to the clearing. The thunder of horses hooves boomed.

"Beth, go back," Henry called, but she didn't listen and within moments, she slammed to the ground, under her attacker's knee, his blade pressed to her throat, watching Henry fight for his life. Watching Henry die.

She cried out in terror as the dream from earlier repeated itself in every horrifying detail. She struggled and fought in vain. She couldn't free herself, couldn't get the gauntlet to Henry. Couldn't save him. Couldn't change the dream.

The battle played out as it had before. As fate intended it.

BETH AWOKE, HOLDING A FAMILIAR WEIGHT in her hands. She panicked. What else could she do?

The adrenalin of fear coursed through her. Her pulse raced. Her head spun and she couldn't think straight. She shot up off the sofa and raced into her tiny kitchen, where she took that horrible, evil glove—and stuffed it into the garbage disposal. Only the fingers would fit, but she listened with satisfaction as the machine's gears tore at the metal digits. The acrid scent of smoke and hot steel stung her nose.

Shaking with body-wrenching spasms, she wrapped the twisted mess in newspaper, foil, and a plastic bag, added a unicorn snow globe paperweight as an anchor then broke the speed limit as she sped to the Di Verdi Lake bridge. She hurled the whole thing over the guardrail with the velocity of a Baseball Hall of Fame star pitcher. It hit the water with a decisive splash.

Still rattled, Beth drove home, oddly focused on how to tell the Camelot Arms' maintenance crew she'd broken the garbage disposal beyond repair.

She took a water-wasting forty-five-minute shower and added to the waterworks with a good long cry once it sank in what she'd done. Sure, the haunted thing had scared the crap out of her, had given her horrible, horrible nightmares, and driven her berserk with its strange powers to...*poof!*...appear out of thin air. But she'd brutalized it and left it to rot with the shopping carts and the rest of the trash on the bottom of the Lake.

And Hal would never forgive her for it.

Chapter Nine

"Beth, wait," Hal called when he saw her come out one of the side doors of Preston North High School, headed for her car.

She jerked to a stop. She wore a dark skirt and a dressy blouse, with her hair hanging loose again, and she eyed him with surprise and what looked like guilt.

The surprise Hal understood. He'd waited here for school to get out and for the students and the buses and the minivans clogging the parent pick-up area of the parking lot to clear out. Waiting, and watching for her to leave. The guilt part he didn't get. *He* should feel guilty for lurking out here like this. Only a desperate man would resort to such a low tactic.

THE FATEFUL KNIGHT

Which he was. Desperate. Last night's dream had turned ugly, and also personal. He'd slipped out of Sir Henry's skin and into his own. He'd called her Beth, not Elizabeth. He'd woken up with his right hand nearly paralyzed and the pain of a thousand swords piercing his gut. He feared the dream realm had begun to splinter and spill into the waking world.

"Beth. I need to talk to you," he said. A couple of teenage girls leaning against the wall nearby put their phones aside and listened in. He took Beth's hand and pulled her around the corner of the building where they could be alone.

"Hal. How did you find me?" she asked, glancing at their entwined hands.

He hastily let go. "You mentioned teaching at the high school. It wasn't hard to figure it out." He looked down and shuffled his feet, unsure how to begin or what to say. "I wanted to apologize for my behavior yesterday. I was way out of line. I was an ass about the money and...everything." He raked his fingers through his hair. "I guess I went overboard.

I'm sure you know how important that armor is to me."

She crossed her arms, a protective gesture, shutting him out. He shifted and tried again.

"I wanted to ask if you'd consider loaning the gauntlet to the museum. It'd still be yours, but it would be on display at the Walker. Lots of people will get a chance to see it, and see Sir Henry as a whole for the first time since..."

He trailed off, gazing at her in silent appeal.

"I can't."

He flinched. "Can't? Or won't?"

"Can't. It's gone."

Storm clouds shrouded his heart. "You sold it?"

"No." She scooped a lock of silky hair behind one ear and stepped back two paces. "I got rid of it. I threw it away."

"*You what?*" His roar seemed to bounce off the school's outer wall and shake the windows. "How could you? You know Sir Henry needs it. *I* need it." He slapped his thighs with his fists. "Where is it? In a dumpster? Where?"

She cringed. Her cheeks burned as red as a raging fire. "It's at the bottom of Di Verdi Lake."

Hal stilled. As still as the grave. Even his blood seemed to stop pumping. "Beth..."

"There's more. I kind of... sort of ground it up in my garbage disposal before I... you know..." She looked away, gazing into the distance with a haunted expression. "Got rid of it."

He said nothing. Couldn't respond. Could only stand there, frozen, crushed. Completely crushed.

"You would have gotten rid of it too," she said, hurrying on. "If you'd seen what I'd seen. Gone through what I went through. I mean, the metal thing not only walked across my apartment, but it broke out of a box. Broke out of a *ton* of bubble wrap. I tried to tell myself I was sleepwalking but how come every time I woke up, there it was, in my arms. I just couldn't take it anymore and I wasn't getting any sleep and—" A tearful hitch caught her voice. "It's cursed. It's *cursed*. It's got some kind of dark magic. I had to get rid of it. I'm sorry, Hal. I feel terrible."

Her words fell from her lips in a confusing, frightened rush. His heart lurched. She looked strained, wrung out, with dark circles under her eyes. Yesterday at the museum, she'd asked him a dozen questions about magic and the armor being haunted. Had she spooked herself with her superstitious questions? Had he added to her fear with his own grim tales, leading her to panic? Or was there something truly supernatural about that damned gauntlet?

Hal ran a hand over his weary face. What did it matter now?

"I guess I'm cursed, too," he said, his voice tight with despair and barely controlled anger. "After all this time, it was within my reach. And it's gone." He searched her face with an intensity he'd never felt before. "Don't you get it? I thought I'd finally found it. Found *you*. I thought fate brought us together and the whole thing was over. I thought Sir Henry could finally have some peace. I thought *I* could have some peace. Now, it's just gonna go on and on. It'll never end. Every night—"

"Miss Astley?" The girls with the phones had followed them and one of them glared at Hal. "Your boyfriend seems pretty pissed. You want us to get help?"

"Tessa, he's not my boyfriend," Beth blurted, as if that were the more important part of Tessa's concern. "It's okay. I'm good." She shooed the girls away.

They left, reluctantly, shooting him suspicious looks. Deserved suspicion. He'd acted like a brute. Like Faintree. Hal's fury fizzled and he stepped back. Time to cut his losses and go.

"I'm sorry, Beth. I'm sorry I bothered you."

He turned and headed for his car, dejected. Whatever the cause, whatever reason had motivated her to do what she did, it was too late. Short of strapping on some scuba diving gear and dredging the bottom of the lake, the gauntlet was gone.

For good.

Chapter Ten

Beth crawled into bed and settled under the covers that night with one hope—no dreams. In particular, no dreams featuring Hal or his medieval twin, Sir Henry. Not even the hot dreams. *Especially* not the hot ones that would only remind her of what she'd lost today. Dreams that would remind her of Hal's expression when he realized she'd destroyed the one thing he prized most in this world. He'd never forgive her and certainly never, ever want to see her again.

She punched her pillow, frustrated and miserable. *When you're wrong, Beth, you're really wrong.* She'd thought, in those heated moments when they'd looked into each other's eyes, that the stars seemed to align. Her heart and her brain had cried, *him... he's The One*. She knew they were right for one another. Call it fate, love at first sight, even reincarnation if the dreams had anything to say about it, but the powerful connection between them felt utterly real.

And now she'd lost him.

She turned on her side and heaved a loud, self-pitying sigh...then closed her eyes.

The night lasted forever. She sobbed, struggled, and moaned, trying to tear out of her subconscious, but the dream trapped her in that nightmare world and the horror repeated over and over again.

The thunder of horses. Men shouted. Metal clanged against metal. Beth as Elizabeth, desperate to break free, to help Henry. Her knight's anguished look as he fell. The hot burn as her attacker dragged his blade across her throat...

This time, when she woke, Beth didn't scream. Terror had stolen her voice. She stared, wide eyed and speechless at the gauntlet.

It shimmered in the morning light, unscarred and whole. Resting on her pillow.

The traffic light ahead winked from green to yellow and Beth floored it before it could turn to red. She didn't dare stop or even slow down as she tore down the city streets toward the Walker Museum.

She glanced at the shoebox with the gauntlet inside on the seat next to her. She'd called in sick from school. Not a lie. She was sick. Dizzy with fear and exhaustion, but finally able to see things clearly. This thing would never leave her alone, never let her rest until she brought it to Sir Henry. That was what the dreams had been trying to tell her. It made sense, in a warped, *Twilight Zone* kind of way. If she reunited the glove with the rest of the armor, maybe, just maybe this ordeal would end.

She turned onto Spencer Street and spotted the Walker ahead, at the top of the rise. A faint rumble rose up far away. Not thunder. Beth knew that now. She recognized the steady, ominous beat from the dream. *Horse's hooves*. Growing louder and steadily closer.

Beth's blood rushed in a frightened flood as she tore into the museum's parking lot. She snatched up the shoebox and dashed toward the front entrance. Her heart sank. The place didn't open until ten and the door was locked. She pounded on the glass until a creaky older man in a guard's uniform sauntered over and glared at her through the thick window.

She begged the man to open the door, her voice wobbling in fear. The thud of hooves behind her intensified, as if a herd of stallions galloped full speed in her direction. As if the villains from the nightmare had leapt into the real world and were coming for her.

To stop her.

"Please open the door," she cried. "I need to see Hal Campion."

That did the trick. The guard fumbled with about a thousand keys on a key ring before the door whisked open.

"Tell Hal to meet me in the Great Hall. *Now*," she called to the guard as she barreled inside and shot up the main staircase. He stared at her blankly, clearly unable to hear the frantic clip-clop of hooves that dogged her. That ghostly torment was meant for Beth's ears alone, apparently.

The Great Hall's chandeliers had been dimmed and the suits of armor stood silently in the darkness. Beth hurried to Sir Henry, making a wide berth around the jousting display, seized by the irrational fear the horse sculptures would spring to life and join the phantom herd pursuing her across the gallery.

She didn't have to wait long before Hal's determined footsteps approached, nearly drowning out the steady beat thrumming in her ears. He wore a long-sleeve shirt, dark pants, and a far from friendly expression. Not to mention far from rested. He looked as bad as she felt, his face pale and drawn, dark circles under his eyes.

"What's the matter?" she blurted.

"Bad dreams." He scrubbed a hand over his face, as if to erase the memory. "What do you want?"

"Peace offering." She opened the shoebox and tipped it, so the gauntlet caught the muted light.

Hal's eyes lit up, but he made no move to touch it. "I thought you said you destroyed it."

"I did. Broke the garbage disposal and everything. I went to bed, had the world's worst nightmare and then this morning, there it sat on my bed like an unwanted guest. As good as new."

He shuddered, gaping in disbelief.

She rushed on. "Remember the other day when I asked you if this..." She gestured to Sir Henry. "If this armor was haunted? Well, I *know* it is. I was trying to tell you that yesterday in my incoherent way. This gauntlet can actually move. Or levitate or beam itself from one place to another or something. I've never seen how it does it, but no matter what I do to it or how far away I get from it, it always comes back to me."

He lifted a hand. "Whoa, slow down. Nightmare?"

She tapped her foot. "That's not important right now. The gauntlet is. I'm telling you, Hal, this thing is *haunted*. I wrapped it in bubble wrap. I threw it in a dumpster. I ground it up in my garbage disposal and drowned it in the lake. But when I woke up, whenever I wake up, there it is, right back in my arms."

He eyed the shoebox and the treasure within, chewing his bottom lip.

"Hal, say you believe me. I'm not making this up and I'm not losing my grip. This is real. Please say you believe me."

He met her gaze and stared at her a long time before he spoke. "I believe you. You're trapped in something... something weird. Something I can't explain but somehow makes perfect sense." He leaned in close. "And you came here today, figuring there's only one way to stop it, to break the curse. To reunite the gauntlet with Sir Henry."

She nodded, flooded with relief. Why hadn't she told him this at the start? He was as solid and understanding as her dad had been. She could trust him, too. "Exactly. Here, it's yours. I don't care about any money or anything. Please, take it."

She held out the shoebox. A tremulous smile touched his lips, mixed with anticipation, as he reached inside the box.

"Son of a—" He snatched back his hand. The glove fell from his grip and hit the floor with a clang that pealed like a broken bell. He blew on his fingers as if they'd been burned. "Apparently *I'm* not destined to ever touch it," he muttered.

She gasped. "You too? I thought the thing burned just me." She bent and scooped it up. The metal singed her fingers, but she'd gotten used to the heat these last few nights. "Try again."

Hal scowled at the gauntlet then at her with equal mistrust and shook his head. "Hard no on that. I think you're supposed to do it."

Like in the dream.

Beth tossed the shoebox to the floor, then stepped closer to the suit of armor. The gauntlet heated her palms to scalding. The sound of hooves, which had lulled these last moments, increased to a volume and tempo that pounded into Beth's brain.

Hal swung a suspicious gaze around the galley. "What is it? What's wrong?"

"It's nothing." Not true, but that explanation could wait for later. Now, she had to make Sir Henry whole.

Jittery, and with the vague fear the knight might suddenly come alive with the final piece of his armor in place, Beth eased the gauntlet over the stump of velvety fabric that stood in for the knight's right hand. The rumble of hoofbeats climbed and climbed and prickles of fear danced along her skin. Hal moved in and rested his hand on her lower back, giving her support. His eyes glimmered and Beth doubted he breathed at all until she'd finished the job.

Hal kept his hand on her back as they gazed at the knight side by side.

And then...nothing. No lightning bolts crashed from the ceiling. Sir Henry didn't suddenly start dancing a jig. The hoofbeats faded back into Beth's imagination where they'd come from.

A giant weight slid off her shoulders. She turned to Hal and grinned, feeling as if she could exhale for the first time in days. They'd done it. Together. They'd put him back together.

"*Finally*. It's over." Hal laughed and impulsively pulled her into a hug, then quickly let her go. "I'll get our conservator to take a look at it this afternoon. She'll connect it to the rest of the armor properly, so it'll be more secure, permanent."

"Permanent. I like the sound of that. No more walking gauntlet. No more bad dreams."

THE FATEFUL KNIGHT

"That's right. I'll be able to get a good night's sleep, for the first time in a year."

"Wait, what? Have you been having dreams too? About Sir Henry and Elizabeth too?"

Hal froze, looking stunned. "Is that what you meant when you said you had a nightmare?"

"Nightmares, plural. Ever since I brought home the gauntlet. Every time I fall asleep."

A horde of what looked like third graders poured into the gallery, accompanied by three harried looking chaperones. The volume of the kids' chatter could've woken the dead.

Hal growled in frustration. "Come with me," he said, his voice grim. "We need to talk."

Chapter Eleven

*H*al took Beth to his office off the third-floor mezzanine. His hands shook so badly he could barely swipe his keycard. *The dreams.* Not only had the gauntlet's bizarre disappearing-then-reappearing magic act besieged Beth, she'd also been tormented by the same dreams about Henry and Elizabeth as him.

Fate roared up and kicked Hal in the teeth. Fate and a large dose of destiny. Fate had drawn them together. Destiny had insisted they return the gauntlet to Sir Henry—together. But what about the dreams? What did they mean? Why were he and Beth having them?

A click and the door lock released. He pulled her into his small, windowless office stuffed with bookcases and several reproduction swords hanging on the wall. He guided her to a chair next to his antique wooden desk littered with books, folders, and plans for future exhibits.

She held the empty shoebox on her lap and gazed up at him expectantly. He scraped his fingers through his hair. Now what? How did he begin what could be a very strange conversation?

"Do you know what that is?" He tipped his head toward a balsa-wood model of a medieval estate on top of one of the bookcases.

"Sir Henry's manor," she said without hesitation. "His, and Elizabeth's."

He pushed some papers aside and leaned on the desk, facing her. His leg brushed her knee. "How do you know that?"

"I know everything about them, because of the dreams. Ever since I got the gauntlet, I've had this...connection to them." She touched her throat and shuddered. "I know how they both died. I've been living through it, as Elizabeth. Hal, it seems so real. It's been a hellish couple of nights."

He shot her a rueful grin. "Try having the same dreams for a year."

Her cheeks paled. "Oh, Hal." She leaned forward and took his hand, giving it a comforting squeeze before she let go. "I didn't know."

"At first, they were mundane. Daily life with Elizabeth, Sir Henry hearing petitions, things like that. We'd just found the *couter* and were looking for the last piece. I thought my dreams were influenced by the search. By my need to finish what Mr. Walker had started. Then I began to dream about Sir Henry's last day, and hers. And what happened at the end."

She winced. "Did they...did they really die that way? In a clearing, ambushed like that?"

"No one knows for sure. But if your dreams are half as realistic as mine—" He grimaced and pressed his palm to a spot below his heart. "Then I think we're living the attack as it really happened."

"But why? Why would Sir Faintree murder them?"

"A lot of reasons. I've lived through enough of Henry's life to know he and Sir Faintree were blood

THE FATEFUL KNIGHT

enemies. Elizabeth was between them. Faintree coveted both her and her land. He planned to murder Henry and marry his grieving widow so he could gain control of her and her estate. But Faintree's own man, in the heat of the attack, foiled that plan by..."

He shrugged, unable to go on.

Beth shook her head. Emotion thickened her voice. "I've only lived in Elizabeth's mind a short time, but I know she would *never* would have married that villain, no matter what. She truly loved Sir Henry." Tears shimmered in her eyes.

"Hey." He pushed off the desk and helped her to stand. The shoebox still on her lap clunked to the floor. He brushed a finger across her cheek, gently wiping away the tears. His hand stilled as he gazed into her eyes. Elizabeth faded from his mind. He saw Beth, and only Beth. The woman fate had brought to him. The woman he wanted to be with. Forever.

"Beth," he murmured.

"Hal," she murmured back. "If ever a moment called for a kiss, it's now."

He laughed softly and did as she suggested. He drew her into his arms. She tipped her head and parted her lips. He cupped her face with both hands and lowered his mouth to hers. She tasted sweet, her lips smooth and supple against his. They melded in a dizzying kiss that set his insides on fire and stole his heart. And far, far better than any dream kiss could ever be.

The first kiss of what he hoped would be many more to come.

They parted, and way too soon.

"I've wanted to kiss you since the moment we met," she said, with an impish grin. "And you didn't disappoint."

He laughed again. Fate had delivered exactly what he needed. Her vibrant spirit and her humor lifted him. The care and stress and dream drama he'd shouldered for the last year melted away.

"Really?" He traced a finger along her lower lip. "I thought you couldn't get away from me fast enough when we met."

"Well, you wanted to steal the gauntlet from me. I had to run away."

THE FATEFUL KNIGHT

"When I thought you were going to sell it to the highest bidder, I *did* think about stealing it."

"I knew it. If I hadn't been arguing with you at the museum at the time in question, I would've thought you were the thief who tried to break into my building."

He frowned. "Thief?"

"Yeah, I thought this guy who tried to buy the gauntlet from me had found out where I lived and come to steal it." She sighed contentedly. "I'm glad it's here now so I don't have to worry about it. I'm glad it's yours now."

He drew her into his arms again. "I'm glad too," he said, still stunned his quest had ended.

She pulled back a bit and rested her palms on his chest. "You know, if I'd just given it to you the other night, I wouldn't have had the dreams. We wouldn't have run into each other again and again."

"I think fate meant for that to happen."

"Fate, coincidence, whatever, I think I was supposed to have the nightmares, supposed to be terrorized by that... that thing, so I could learn how important it was to Sir Henry and to you. And to understand how important you are to me."

She smiled and tipped her head back, inviting another kiss. He obliged, kissing her deeply, more demanding, holding her and never wanting to let go. His heart hammered and happiness filled his soul.

The dreams were done. The ghosts of Henry and Elizabeth had been put to rest. And he could move on.

With Beth.

HAL STEPPED OUT OF THE FIRST-FLOOR conference room after a budget meeting that had dragged on for what felt like weeks. He glanced out the window. Outside, storm clouds had rolled in, giving the afternoon a gray, gloomy tinge, but the threat of rain didn't dampen his spirits. He grinned. No dull meeting or bad weather could bring him down now.

He had a date with Beth tonight.

Hal headed down the hallway and climbed the stairs to the Great Hall, happier and more hopeful than he'd been in a long time. They'd talked for an

THE FATEFUL KNIGHT

hour in his office this morning, kissed for almost as long, and made a date for tonight as Hal walked her to her car. He would pick Beth up after he left work, for dinner... and whatever. His breath caught every time he thought about what *whatever* could entail.

His footsteps echoed as he entered the strangely silent and empty main gallery. A tweak of foreboding scratched at the back of his mind. The Great Hall typically wasn't mobbed on a weekday, but they usually had school groups moving through all day, chattering, laughing, and making tons of noise.

He steered toward Sir Henry's corner, to check on the conservator's progress with securing the final piece to the knight's armor. A hulking figure suddenly shot out of the shadows and reached for the gauntlet.

"Hey, stop," Hal shouted, sprinting the rest of the way.

The man swung around, and Hal recoiled as if he'd taken a battering ram to the gut. Beefy and muscular, with a hatchet face and a thick black beard, the man wore a wool tunic and leggings—and could've been Sir Faintree's clone.

Or his ghost.

"I need this," the man gritted and lunged for the armor again.

Hal dove to stop him and the two men touched the gauntlet at the same time. Molten heat seared Hal's palm and he bit off an agonized curse. The bearded man was burned worse—acrid smoke curled up from his charred fingers.

A moment later, a crack of thunder, a blinding flash, and the gauntlet exploded in a burst of fire that rattled the windows and blew Hal off his feet. He crashed down on his back a dozen feet away. The explosion threw Faintree's double into the air and he hit the floor with a reverberating thud.

Hal had no time to think. Faintree scrambled to his feet and advanced toward Sir Henry once more. Hal dashed after him but skidded to a stop when the smoke around the armor cleared.

The gauntlet had vanished.

THE FATEFUL KNIGHT

HAL GAPED AT THE EMPTY SPACE. "Holy sh—"

Faintree cut him off with a hard, fast clip to the jaw. Hal sprawled on the floor for a second time, seeing stars. His opponent pounded out of the gallery. Hal got up, shoved the pain and confusion from his brain and ran after him.

Seconds later, outside the museum, he searched around frantically. The fake Faintree was gone. Vanished. How, Hal didn't know. Where the man was headed, Hal did.

He jumped into his car and squealed out of the museum's parking lot. Dark, ominous clouds shot across the sky, pushed by a strong gust of wind, seeming to chase him. He fumbled with his phone, desperate to punch in a number. He ran a red light and swerved to pass a slow-moving car.

"C'mon, c'mon, answer," he said through gritted teeth as his clumsy thumb finally connected and the phone rang. *God's blood!* His call went to voicemail.

Hal shot a worried glance behind him. The clouds had thickened, turning dark and swollen with danger. The wind howled and thunder roared. He gripped the steering wheel so tight his knuckles whitened. His earlier tweak of foreboding erupted into a full-on disaster alarm.

Hal slammed the gas pedal to the floor and his car shot down the darkening street. He had to stop the bearded man. He knew where the fake Faintree was going.

To Beth.

Chapter Twelve

*B*eth floated into her apartment and closed the door, tossing her keys in the direction of the small table holding a barely thriving spider plant.

What a difference a few hours could make. She'd fled her apartment this morning, fearful and frantic. She returned several hours later, grinning and giddy. After three days of overheated, tossing and turning nightmares and being haunted by that strange gauntlet, it had finally found its home.

And she had a date tonight with Hal, a true knight in shining armor if there ever was one. And an awesome kisser.

She could hardly believe this was happening. Then again, it seemed inevitable. They were a perfect fit. She didn't put as much faith in fate as Hal did, but something seemed to have thrown them together. She liked to think her dad had taken a hand in her destiny, looking on from above. He wouldn't want her to keep mourning. He'd want her to move on with her life and be happy. And now she was.

She yawned. Happy, but exhausted. A power nap would do her a world of good. Freshen her up for her date tonight, too. After a quick lunch of grilled cheese and grape jelly—her favorite comfort food—Beth settled in for a snooze.

A MUTED RUMBLE OF THUNDER GAVE WAY to that sound she'd come to dread. Massive black horses crashed into the clearing, snorting, stamping their muscular legs as their riders reined them in.

No. Not possible. Somehow, she'd gotten pulled into the nightmare again.

Her gaze flew to Henry standing by the boulder. Their eyes met a brief, desperate moment. He opened his mouth, but no words came out. Instead, a high-pitched chirp, like a choir of crickets...

Beth blinked. Blinked again. That insistent chirp came from her phone by her bed, tearing her out of her nightmare. *Thank goodness for small favors.*

"Beth," a man's voice blurted when she answered, anxious and out of breath. "I'm on my way to you. I'm almost there."

"What?" She passed a hand over her eyes, trying to shake free of the sleep cobwebs still clogging her brain. "Hal...? Is it time for our date?"

"Listen, Beth. The gauntlet's gone. Your bearded friend was here. He tried to... Look, there's no time to explain. I'm almost to your place, but so is he." Panic laced his voice. "Just get out of your apartment. I want you safe— Beth? Are you there?"

Tightly gripping the phone, she slowly turned her head.

The gauntlet lay on her pillow.

Chapter Thirteen

The next moments shot by in a terrifying blur.

Beth's apartment door crashed open. The bearded man lurched into her bedroom. She screamed. She heard Hal on the phone. He called out to her in a terrified voice. She snatched up the gauntlet and scrambled from her bed. She tried to dash by the intruder, but he grabbed her hair and yanked her to a painful stop.

He pulled her against him and clamped a hand crisscrossed with burns over her mouth. His foul scent stung her nose. "The gauntlet," he growled. "Give it to me, my lady."

Damn this hunk of metal.

Beth would gladly let him have it. The thing grew hotter by the second, rapidly heating, burning her fingers. But she couldn't hand it over. Something wouldn't let her. Some force or impulse made her keep the glove close, clutched protectively to her breast. She could only give it to Hal. And no one else. Especially not this smelly guy crushing her in his bruising hold.

She stomped down hard on the man's instep and jabbed an elbow into his side. He grunted and loosened his grip, just enough to allow her to push out of his creepy embrace and run.

Shouting for help, she sprinted to the door. It hung askew, its hinges broken and torn from the doorjamb when Beard Man had broken through. Hal raced into her apartment from the hallway at the moment Beth reached the door. She bashed into him. Her assailant, running hot on her heels, smacked into them both and they all sprawled to the floor.

The gauntlet flew from Beth's hold and skidded across the floor. She scrambled after it on hands and knees. So did Hal. The bearded man lunged toward it and all three touched the red-hot metal at the same time.

A burst of lightning shot out of the glove like a sizzling fireball. An explosion rocked Beth's apartment. Smoke blinded her. The force of the blast flung her sideways and she banged against something solid.

She blacked out.

An instant later—or perhaps eons—Beth opened her eyes. She looked around, groggy, confused, trying to focus. The scent of damp earth hung in the air. She lay back against... what? She felt behind her, touching something soft, like peach fuzz. Moss. She sat against a tree with a thick trunk, like all the other trees that surrounded this clearing.

Fear chilled her blood. She'd been dragged back into her nightmare. Only this time she was Beth, not Elizabeth. She had no idea how she knew that. She just did.

Then she saw him. The knight. He stood at the other end of the clearing by the boulder, his back to her. He swung around and she gasped. Not Sir Henry this time.

The knight was Hal.

He looked at her with a dazed expression. "Beth, I don't think this is a dream. This is real."

About to move toward her, he stopped and cocked his head, listening. She heard it too, a rhythmic thud deep in the woods. Horses, closing in. Hal's expression morphed from stunned to agonized. His dream, her dream, their dream was coming true.

The riders drew closer. Beth tried to scramble to her feet, but she could barely move. The lightning or explosion or whatever had knocked them into this never-ending medieval horror movie had zapped her nerve endings, draining her of strength.

"Hal, your helmet," she shouted.

He hastily scooped up the helmet from the top of the boulder and put it on. He reached for his sword and his hand stilled—only the thinnest of leather gloves protected his forearm.

Stupefied, Beth looked down and saw that she held the gauntlet in a strangling grip.

"I need it. *Now*," Hal cried, his voice strained, muffled by his helmet.

Beth struggled upward, moving with great effort, as if she pushed through a vat of tar. She managed to stand on wobbly legs and slowly inched toward Hal.

Three mounted men crashed through the brush into the clearing. She jerked sideways to avoid being trampled by the panting beasts as their riders circled her. The putrid odor of man and horse stung her nostrils and she stumbled, tangled in the folds of her heavy skirt, but she stayed focused on Hal.

He must've been terrified, but he unsheathed his sword and held it ready in his vulnerable right hand. As in the dream, their foes leapt off their horses and attacked. The *ting* of metal on metal sounded through the clearing as the men joined in battle.

Hal swiveled and parried and thrust, holding his own. The man without armor fell with a scream, stabbed in the gut. Sir Faintree barely paused at his cohort's demise and lunged at Hal full force.

"Come on, Hal. You've got this," Beth whispered, more hopeful than sure.

Her own attacker surged at her. In a moment, she would be pinned under his bulk and the brutal

THE FATEFUL KNIGHT

sequence of dream events would unspool. She squeezed the scalding metal, her panic suddenly swallowed by anger. It didn't have to happen this way. Beth had accepted the fact she couldn't save her father, but she could save Elizabeth.

Would fate allow her to change the rules?

She took a breath and forced herself to wait a precious second. When her attacker reached for her, she shoved the gauntlet in his face. The glove's metal fingers stabbed into his eyes like hot pokers.

He screeched in pain and buckled to the ground, clawing at his eyes.

She shot a frantic glance at Hal. His blade flew as he held off the villainous Sir Faintree, but he backed up with each parry, moving closer to the boulder, closer to being trapped. Beth had escaped Elizabeth's killer, surely Hal could escape Sir Henry's fate, too.

If he had what he needed.

She didn't hesitate another second. She dashed toward Hal as he crashed against the boulder. Faintree raised his sword.

"Hal," she called and chucked the gauntlet toward him. It arced upward slightly and clunked onto the rock's narrow lip, where it teetered, balancing precariously.

Hal moved swiftly. He dropped his sword, swiveled, jammed the glove onto his hand and scooped up his blade in one smooth, balletic motion. Surprised, Faintree staggered, and his sword sliced the air. Hal used this brief reprieve to get his bearings. He crouched, then stabbed up and sideways, aiming for the same chink in his opponent's armor that felled Sir Henry.

Faintree howled in anger and agony, but Hal showed no mercy. He stabbed again and the villain fell with a thud.

Hal sagged back against the big rock as if stunned. But only a moment. He dropped his sword, tore off his helmet, and closed the short distance between them. Breathing hard, his hair matted to his scalp from sweat, he pulled Beth into his arms and crushed her to him. She felt his body shaking through his armor. Adrenaline, fear, and an overwhelming sense of relief surged through her too, making Beth tremble twice as much as Hal.

They stood holding one another for a long, long time.

"Hal..." she murmured, tears coursing down her cheeks. "You're alive. You're alive."

"You saved me, Beth." He gave her a breath-stopping squeeze then released her. "We cheated fate. And I finally defeated him." He bent over Faintree's still form and, with a growl, tugged off his helmet. The bearded man's dark eyes stared vacantly up at them.

"Hal, it's him."

"I'm not surprised. It fits." He looked around the clearing, squinting in disbelief. "Everything fits." He looked back at her and smiled. "And we fit, my lady."

He drew her into his arms again and pressed his lips to hers in a desperate, all-consuming kiss that lasted a moment, or forever, or somewhere in between. Beth couldn't tell. She only knew Hal's kiss was perfect. Sweet and passionate and absolutely perfect.

When they parted, they were in her apartment, in their own time, in the clothes they'd been wearing when time or fate or whatever strange force had swept them up and transported them into the dream world.

"What about Sir Faintree?" Beth gazed anxiously around the living room, but Beard Man had disappeared. "Where did he go?"

"I don't know."

"Who was he? Was he having the dreams too?"

"Or maybe he was part of the dream," Hal mused. "A ghost whose mission was to make sure we didn't get the gauntlet."

"Or maybe the opposite. Maybe it was fate again, using the gauntlet to bring us together. I thought fate was working against us, but I think it wanted us to fight, and to somehow *help* Sir Henry. For us to right a terrible wrong and change the past. To change history. And save Henry and Elizabeth." She shivered, frightened by her own words, overwhelmed by what had just happened. "It wasn't a dream this time, was it?"

Hal shrugged then winced. "My arms and shoulders hurt like hell." He took her hand and kissed her scorched and blistered fingers. "These burns are real."

He scanned her apartment, searching the floor, but it wasn't there. Somehow, Beth knew it wouldn't be.

"I think it's where it belongs," she said. "If we really did change the past, then the gauntlet is with Sir Henry. Where it should've been all this time."

Hal's lips curved in a mystified grin. "I know one thing for a fact. I'm glad I paid attention in fencing class. I also think we owe fate or destiny or whatever a hearty thanks. It brought us together. It sure used unconventional means to do it, but..."

He pulled her into his embrace again.

"My lady, I think we're fated to be together for a very long time."

Epilogue

Beth's phone chirped. Her heart raced to hear Hal on the other end of the line when she answered. Amazing how just the sound of his voice could do that.

It had been almost three weeks since their trip through time, or "our boring first date" as Hal liked to call it. They'd been together day and night since then and not a single bad dream or bearded man or a glint of a gauntlet had bothered them.

"Can you come over to the museum before we close?" Hal asked.

"Sure, I can leave as soon as the maintenance guy is done." Beth glanced toward the man in olive-green overalls who'd stuffed his considerable

THE FATEFUL KNIGHT

bulk under her sink to replace her busted garbage disposal. "Why, what's up?"

"I want to show you something special. It's a new acquisition. Meet me in the main gallery."

A half hour later, she left the Camelot Arms, enduring yet another disapproving glare from her neighbor, Mrs. Parkhurst, who sat on a lawn chair on the front stoop.

It had taken a lot of convincing to get the old woman and her other neighbors to believe Beth's busted door and screams for help the day Faintree's ghost had attacked her were a simple misunderstanding. Since Beard Man had vanished without a trace, Mrs. Parkhurst blamed Hal for the ruckus and she threatened to bash him with her broom every time she saw him for scaring everyone like that.

Probably a good time to move. Beth wondered if King Arthur Commons on the other side of town had any apartments open. For her and her knight.

She entered the Great Hall moments later and found Hal near the jousting display. He gave her a welcoming grin that made her temperature flame to critical. Resisting the urge to fan herself, Beth followed him to the east wall, where a gaggle of visitors had gathered to watch several of Hal's co-workers use a pulley system to hoist a heavy tapestry up onto the wall.

Despite the worn fabric and the once-brilliant colors now faded, the tapestry's embroidered images teemed with immediacy and life. The scene depicted a small crowd gathered near a castle's outer wall, waving to a mounted knight as he set out on his journey. He wore armor, except for his helmet held rakishly under his arm. His youthful vigor hadn't faded a bit over time, except for the threads of silver through his raven hair.

"Sir Henry?" Beth asked.

Hal slid his arm around her waist and gave her a quick kiss on the cheek. "That's him. And there's his lady."

He gestured to Elizabeth, who stood looking up at her knight with a loving smile. Time had washed out the vivid green of her dress and her red hair had faded, but the image captured Elizabeth's spirit and strength in vibrant detail.

According to historical records, Henry had lived a long and fruitful life. So had Elizabeth. They'd had more children, many adventures, and many, many years together. Beth and Hal had changed the past, somehow. And they had changed the future for themselves. They'd put to rest the grief and regrets that had troubled them both and followed their destinies.

As fate had wanted.

"And look there." Hal tightened his hold around Beth's waist as he pointed, directing her gaze to Elizabeth, reaching up to Sir Henry's outstretched hand.

She gave him his gauntlet.

~ The End ~

I hope you enjoyed reading *The Fateful Knight* as much as I did writing it. Please help others find this story by leaving a review.

And don't forget to visit my website for more information on me and my books, including the adventures of feisty time traveling librarian Beryl

Blue in the award-winning *Beryl Blue, Time Cop* time travel series. While you're there, please take a moment to sign up for my newsletter for updates on what I'm working on, plus exclusive content, free books, and other goodies.

Just stop by my website to join the fun! www.janetrayestevens.com

Now, as an extra bonus, here's a sneak peek of BERYL BLUE, TIME COP, the first book in time traveling librarian Beryl Blue's series of adventures. Enjoy!

BERYL BLUE, TIME COP

"A perfect blend of historical fiction, a bit of sci-fi, and wonderful romance. A really fun read."

Feisty librarian Beryl Blue is hurled from 2015 to WWII, tasked with stopping a time traveling assassin from killing a soldier on leave and changing history forever. The bad guy is one problem, his target is another. Beryl's stunned to find herself falling for sexy, stubborn Army sergeant Tom 'Sully' Sullivan, who makes it abundantly clear he can take care of himself.

With an assassin on their heels and all of history on her shoulders, Beryl scrambles to protect a man who refuses to be protected—and keep her heart intact.

Chapter One

"**B**eryl Blue, Time Cop," I shouted. "Stop!"

The guy I chased didn't. Didn't even slow down. Which put me in A Mood, as Grandma Blue had called my teenaged temperament. But who could blame me for getting annoyed? My ankle still bitched from last week's not-so-fun run in 1599, chasing that guy stalking Shakespeare. The trip through the temporal gate today had been its usual shake-and-bake fun. Now here I was in 1977, running after an overdue time tourist on a steamy hot July afternoon.

While wearing a policewoman's uniform with a worsted wool jacket and skirt.

And pantyhose.

What's more, the time-perp I pursued zipped along on roller skates. Sprinting after him made my ankle throb like the dickens.

"Come on, man," I called. "Stop!"

The guy pumped his chalky legs harder, picking up speed. His skate wheels rumbled as he zigzagged around pedestrians. He was cruising for a close encounter with my cack .28, and I was going to oblige. Time Scope Excursions had a whole list of rules for time tourists, but number one was to come home when your vacation in the past had ended. No exceptions.

That's where I came in. My job was to find and extract overdue time tourists any way necessary.

I slipped the weapon out of its holster and armed it. My quarry skated into the clear. I aimed. The guy fell. Not from the cack's invisible burst of scorching juice. From a crack. In the sidewalk. Flew ass over teakettle and landed flat on his squishy butt. To my relief, and to the delight of Hampton Beach's feathery-hairdo crowd, who cheered his triple-gainer wipeout.

I holstered the cack and limped over to him. He grimaced up at me. Would've been comical if he didn't look so pathetic, splayed like a starfish in his disco roller boogie outfit, his short shorts riding up high enough for all 1977 to get a good look at his package.

I averted my eyes. I'm dainty that way.

"You wouldn't have caught me if I didn't trip," he said, sitting up and wincing in pain.

"Seriously? I would've killed you." I tapped my holster for emphasis. Time Scope didn't fool around. Better to take out a rogue time tourist than have them upset the timeline by running wild in the past.

I helped the guy to stand. He wobbled like a newborn colt until he got his balance.

"Please, ma'am, don't bring me back," he said. Begged, really.

"Ma'am?" Yikes. I was twenty-four, still got carded everywhere I went. This guy was pushing forty. "Do I look like your grandmother?"

"I'm sorry, ma'am, uh, officer. But, please, don't take me back. I don't *belong* in 2130."

Oh, crap. He was one of *them*. A runner. He hadn't stepped through one of Time Scope's temporal gates to go on an expensive vacation, or even with a nefarious plan to loot the treasures of the past.

He'd intended his time trip to be only one way. He'd intended to disappear into history.

"That's what they all say," I muttered, avoiding his pleading eyes, because—irony alert—I didn't belong in 2130 either. Six months ago, I was a happy wannabe librarian living my life in the early 21st century. Well, sort of happy. Okay, pretty miserable if truth be told. But the thing was, I could never, ever go back to that time. "And, seriously, 1977? I mean, *Star Wars* comes out, I get that. But of all the time periods in all of history, why run here? Why now?"

"I love the music. And..." He sniffed the air. "You smell that? What is it? It's heavenly."

I'd caught the smell too, had packed on five pounds just from the aroma. "Fried dough."

His milky blue eyes lit up. "Fried dough," he said with reverence, then his voice cracked with sudden panic. "Please don't take me back. Say you killed me. Say anything. *Please* let me stay."

This guy hit new levels of pathetic, going straight for my heart. Guess he didn't get the memo. I used to let emotions guide me. Not anymore. Glo Reid, Time Scope and a lying guy named Jake Tyson had seen to that. Now I was nothing but a cold-hearted company goon.

At least, that's what I kept telling myself.

"Look, disco man," I said, harsher than I intended. I would *not* let this pathetic puppy get to me. "You *can't* stay. A skate down the sidewalk in 1977 won't change anything, but if you disappear into the past? The future. Is. Screwed. So, no way I'm leaving you here, *capiche*?"

My bad ass act seemed to scare him more than threatening him with the weapon. He came along quietly when I suggested we find a spot where we could disappear without witnesses. I towed him away from the beach toward the bustling downtown, looking for an alley. He gazed wistfully at the boat-sized cars clogging the street, the people dressed in colors that would make Joseph's *Technicolor Dreamcoat* look subdued, and the stores advertising wares still made in the USA.

"Wait." I stopped, spotting a sale sign in a store window. I felt a smile coming on. I hadn't smiled in a while. It felt good. "A quick stop, then back home and off to the cage with you."

"That's contraband," my prisoner cried when he saw where we were headed. "I'll tell unless you let me go."

"No, you won't." I patted my holster again and he shut up. But to be on the safe side, I decided to invest in a big piece of fried dough for his enjoyment before we went back to the future.

"You bucking for Time Cop of the year, Beryl?" Carmine slapped the buzzer and the holding cage door clanged sideways. "That's the third temporal ex-pat you brung in this month."

I shrugged. "It's an epidemic."

Carmine scratched his salt-and-pepper mustache then dug into his ear for good measure. "I don't get why anyone would run to an earlier time. We got everything you could ever want here."

"I know, right?" I adjusted the package in the brown paper bag tucked under my arm. Not *every*thing.

I signaled to my disco friend to wipe fried dough crumbs off his face then pushed him into the cell.

He rolled across the tile, and I held my breath as he tripped-fell onto a bench. The guy had been through enough without the added indignity of face planting in front of Time Scope's second shift. The cell door slid shut and I turned away from his sad blue eyes.

Poor guy. He'd be off to rehab in the morning. Not the kind of rehab anyone from my 21st century home would recognize. No twelve steps, no daily affirmations. It was a quick fix that involved some kind of laser lobotomy. The guy would be all happy-happy, joy-joy and would never want to roller boogie in another time period again.

I pushed the guy's brain-scrambling fate out of my mind. What he'd done was dangerous. I cringed to think what could've happened to the historical timeline if I hadn't caught him.

After what seemed like weeks of paperwork, I returned my 1970s cop uniform to wardrobe and changed into jeans and a windbreaker. I tucked my contraband into my backpack and took a Metro-Slide home in the fading daylight of an April afternoon. The lights in my high-rise studio apartment popped on as I entered. Jenjen, my monstrous Maine coon cat, met me at the door. I took off my jacket and hefted my backpack onto the kitchen counter, pushing aside a stack of books. Jenjen leapt up with impressive agility for such a fat cat and stuck his face into the backpack as I unzipped it.

"That's not for you." I pushed him away and pulled out a six-pack of Budweiser.

I'd broken one of Time Scope's many rules—no souvenirs. But it wasn't like the powers that signed my paycheck dared to squawk. After everything I'd gone through on the company's behalf, they owed me. Big time.

I slipped my finger through the ring-tab on one of the beer cans and popped the top. The beer was foamy from the time trip, but still cold.

"Can't get beer like this here in 2130," I said, taking a sip and scratching behind Jenjen's ear. "Not without a prescription, anyway."

He twitched his tail, a signal in any century that said, "Not interested. Feed me."

A bowl of kitty chow later, he washed his paws contentedly as I settled into my chair and started on my own dinner, the second can of my contraband six pack.

"Entertainment Communications Interface," I said, resting my sore ankle on a footstool. A portion of my apartment's west wall dissolved at my command to reveal a giant TV screen. Several function icons popped up. "Music." The icons faded, except for the G-clef, which blossomed in size. "World War Two mix. Random."

The aching, melancholy "I'll Be Seeing You," sung by Rosemary Clooney, softly filled the air. My heart wrenched as the memories rushed in like a flood tide. I thought of the roller boogie disco man and the music he loved. Music that made him give up everything to flee to another time. I didn't get his passion for the thumping '70s disco beat, but I got where the passion came from. I'd risk everything, too, if I could go back to that one moment, forget about the timeline, and just go.

Go to *him*.

Before I could stop myself, I had the photograph in my hand. I'd never uploaded it to the Interface. I didn't want anyone else to get access to it, whether by accident or design. I wanted it where only I could see it, only I could hold it. I'd tucked the photo into a drawer in my bedside table, promising myself I'd only look at it once a month.

Yesterday. I'd made that promise yesterday.

"What can I say, Sully?" I murmured, gazing at the photo. "I'm weak."

There they were, in glorious four-by-five black-and-white. Four GIs crowded around a small table littered with beer bottles and shot glasses, looking like the cast of a John Wayne World War II movie. Marco, Griff, Stan...

And Sully.

I slid my thumb over Sully's face. I longed to stroke that impossibly strong jaw for real. To touch that Grand Canyon-deep chin cleft. Run my fingers through his thick, copper-red hair. A cigarette dangled from his lips, as usual. Smoke coiled around his eyes, making him squint. He was smiling. The one honest, happy moment before he shipped out. Before places like Normandy and Bastogne. Before the terrible events that tore us apart forever.

I was in the picture, perched on Sully's lap. I looked pretty. I was smiling too. Really smiling. I was so soft then. Not my body. I'd always been a solid size fourteen. My heart was soft. Sully had his arm around my waist, his free hand rested on my leg. I could almost feel his touch, his hand on my thigh, his fingers gently massaging. The ache in my heart doubled.

I had to stop doing this, had to stop pining for a memory and longing for a man I could never be with. A man I'd lost long ago.

I reached for another can and popped the top on my third beer, hoping the buzz beginning to cloud my brain would help me forget.

Forget, for just a little while.

How did a librarian from 2015 end up as a time cop in the twenty second century? Find out in the first book of Beryl's adventures, *Beryl Blue, Time Cop*

Meet author Janet Raye Stevens

Mom, reader, tea-drinker (okay, tea guzzler), and teller of hilarious and sometimes totally true tales. Derringer and Silver Falchion Award finalist and winner of RWA's Golden Heart® and Daphne du Maurier awards, Janet writes historical mysteries, time travel adventures, and the occasional Christmas romance, all with humor, heart, and a dash of suspense. She lives, writes, and drinks copious amounts of tea at her home in New England.

Made in United States
North Haven, CT
21 November 2024